TRUST ME

TRUST ME

Rajashree

Rupa & Co

Typeset in Times New Roman by
Nikita Overseas Pvt. Ltd.
1410 Chiranjiv Tower
43 Nehru Place
New Delhi 110 019

Printed in India by
Rekha Printers Pvt. Ltd.
A-102/1 Okhla Industrial Area, Phase-II
New Delhi-110 020

*Dedicated
to my grandparents,
Kushuajji, Biraji, Vahini and Babu,
with all my love*

THANK YOU!

I would like to thank

Aai, for being the wind beneath my wings.

Manju, who led the way. Bunty, for being a pillar of strength. Prayas, who's inspired me with his creative energy and mast kalandar-ness.

Jyoti Dogra, Sachin Krishn and Shailesh Gupta, my closest friends, for sharing my laughter and my tears.

Jyothi Kapur Das. She's read each and every draft of the manuscript, edited it and even written a lot of witty lines. I hope her sense of humour and joie de vivre are inherited by her babies – Bubu, Guddu and her films.

The team at Rupa for their enthusiasm about *Trust Me*. Ruskin Bond and Shinie Antony, for liking the manuscript. Deepthi Talwar for her clarity and professionalism. Bharati Chopra, who's helped me with my nukhtachini. Kapish Mehra, for his energy and marketing savvy.

Kiran Nagarkar, Michele Roberts, Rachel Holmes, Sean Mahoney, Annette Green, Isobel Dixon, Shubhra Krishan, Randhir Khare and Meher Pestonjee, for helping me fine-

tune the manuscript. Laxmikant Shetgaonkar and Sandhya
Gokhale, friends and fellow-writers, who were a great source
of ideas and encouragement.

My friends who read the manuscript and excerpts from
it at various stages and gave me invaluable feedback. It's
a long list, and I feel very grateful to have so many lovely
people in my life. Here they are, alphabetically :-). Arti
Sharma, Chirantan Das, Kamal Paranjape, Mannu Kohli,
Mansoor Khan, Munnu Chourse, Pankaj Rishi Kumar, Pervin
Mahoney, Prashant Narayanan, Purab Kohli, Ravi
Deshpande, Rita Agarwal, Rohit Patel, Ruchika Oberoi,
Rupali Saxena Bhattacharjee, Sagar Ballary, Sai Prasen,
Saikat Ghosh, Sankalp Meshram, Savita Patel, Vijay
Phanshikar...

Kunjan Mendke, for her strength – and her vulnerability.
Kumkum, Radhika and Chandni Kapur, the warmest and
most hospitable people I've ever met. Narain (who-used-
to-be-Sunil!), my cute phone-friend. Rajendra Chourse,
who has always been there whenever I've needed sound
advice. Mukund Pagey, for our regular Saturday morning
calls.

R. Sriram and Harish Shenoy, for sharing their insights
about publishing with me. Ashima Narain, Ashok Purang,
Balakrishna Pillai, Dionne Bunsha, Kshitij Negi, Kunal
Jhaveri, Madhusudan Banhatti, Murzban Shroff, Pankaj
Kumar, Piyush Mishra, Pratik Basu, Sarnath Banerjee, Vikas
Kumar and Vikram Kapadia, who helped me in the run-up
to the release of the book. Chetan Sharma, Romel Dias,
Gayatri Rao and Prajakta Sansare, for designing such a
bright, happy cover.

Surendra Gokhale and Bhushan Banhatti, for those hazaar printouts. Reliable Xerox Centre, Fort, and Allwyn Jumbo Xerox, Andheri – I've spent so much time in these shops that my sister had nicknamed me 'Xerox and Typing'.

The Film and Television Institute of India, my alma mater. Gloria Koshy, for giving me a room with a view where this novel was born. Sagheer Ahmed, my scriptwriting teacher.

You, dear Reader! I hope this book touches your heart as well as makes you laugh. A lot.

ONE

Bombay.

Coming back to Bombay felt like an assault on the senses. Thud. Thud. Thud. The coolies started jumping into the train even before it had come to a halt. They squeezed their way through the crowded door which was packed with passengers waiting to get off. I glared at a coolie who brushed past my breasts but he had no time to even look at me. I cursed myself. I should've sat quietly on my seat till everybody else had got off. Victoria Terminus was the last station, the train wasn't going to be running off anywhere. But no, I had to crowd into the passage with everybody pressing into each other like it were a local train.

I turned to avoid the strong smell of chameli that wafted from the hair of the woman standing in front of me. As it is, my head had started aching because of the pollution by the time our train crossed Dombivali.

'Don't push,' I snapped at the man behind me who was digging his suitcase into the back of my legs.

'Then move quickly, no!'

Everybody was in a hurry, but in typical Bombay fashion, nobody was getting anywhere. The roads were flooded and a bus had stalled in front of the station, blocking the traffic. It was March, it wasn't supposed to be raining. It wasn't supposed to be so hot so soon, either. But it was.

I looked at my watch once again. It was one and a half hours since I had reached V.T. One hour of being squashed in the rush-hour crush of the local train from V.T. to Andheri. Plus half an hour of waiting for the bus. The only thing to feel grateful about was that I was protected from the rain by the bus shelter, unlike the men who were out on the street in knee-deep water, pushing the stalled bus. It seemed like an impossible task, but finally, they managed to move it enough to let the auto-rickshaws and two-wheelers pass. I decided that for once, I could allow myself the luxury of an auto, so I hiked my salwar above my knees, picked up my suitcases and stepped out into the rain.

I hadn't realised that the queue for the autos was so long. Seventeen people in the line and not one available auto. There wasn't even any shelter here, so I just stood in the pouring rain, shifting my weight from one foot to the other. I desperately needed to go to the loo. There was a McDonald's right in front of me, and I was damned hungry as well, but I didn't want to lose my place in the auto line. All I wanted was to get back to my place. Just my 'place', not my home, I wouldn't call it home, in fact I didn't really have... Oh, shut up, Paro! I watched in utter frustration as the bus I'd been waiting for passed by peacefully, splashing mud on all the idiots standing in the rain, waiting for autos, the biggest idiot in the world being, obviously, me.

I hated the lipstick-stained cigarette butts my room-mate left around the place almost as much as I hated the smell of stale smoke hanging in the air. Did she have an allergy to fresh air or what?

I banged the windows open. But it didn't make much difference to Shweta. She probably thought the banging was part of Metallica. If there was one thing I couldn't stand in life, it was heavy metal music. I'd given up asking her to turn down the volume. Her fundas were clear – she also paid two thousand rupees a month, she was entitled to play music if she felt like. And, as she never tired of reminding me, she'd been staying here long before I'd come on the scene.

So here I was, paying two thousand rupees a month for this dingy little room which had come with one double bed, five Godrej almirahs and one Shweta. 'Four-four mirrors. Very nice room,' the estate agent had grinned when he first brought me here. I'd told him hesitantly that I didn't need four mirrors or even five almirahs, but it turned out that the landlady wanted them there to store her own things. Shweta and I had to keep our clothes in a wooden rack that covered half the window. Not that we missed the view – the window looked out onto an open sewer that flowed by, two floors below. The worst thing about the room was that we had to sleep together on the bed. But what could I do? This was the only place I'd been able to find when I came to Bombay nine months ago.

At least we had an attached bathroom. The cold shower on my body felt like a blessed relief. I could have stood there forever, enveloped in the translucent cocoon that alienated me from everything around, even the pounding of the music... Was that the music or was someone banging...? I turned the shower off and peeped out of the door.

'Your boss on the line,' Shweta shouted over the music.

I quickly rubbed myself dry and then had to get back into my dirty wet salwar kameez. The phone was in the drawing room and the landlady had made a rule that we were not to wear our nighties outside our room.

'He'd called a couple of times when you were out of town. I forgot to tell you,' Shweta said.

'Thanks,' I said sarcastically, below my breath.

'Hello, sir, sorry to have kept you waiting, sir. I just got back...'

'Paro! How are you?' the warm voice boomed out.

'Fine, I'm fine,' I said, adjusting my dupatta. The landlord was staring at me from the side of his newspaper. Maybe the landlady had a point there, about not wearing nighties outside our room.

'What happened?' Mr Bose said. 'Raghu told me that you left in the middle of the Silkina Moisturiser shoot because you couldn't cope, just started crying. What's the matter?'

'I... uh... just some personal problem, sir.'

'What is it? Is there anything I can do?'

'No... I don't know...' The unexpected help made me want to start crying.

'Tell you what, why don't you meet me for dinner tonight? There's this place near where you stay... Your phone number starts with 2624, that's Andheri, isn't it? Serves really nice Mexican stuff. Nothing like a good meal to make everything feel alright.'

One look at Mr Bose and you could tell that he really believed that. He looked like he ate well, and the food gave him not just calories, but also a sense of well-being that radiated from him as he heaped enchiladas on my plate, urging me to forget about dieting-vieting, Indian men liked plump women in real life. Models just looked good on screen. He should've known – he was one of the best-paid ad film-makers in the country.

I was quite touched by his concern, actually. I was just an assistant production designer in his company. Everybody talked about how the office was like 'one big family', and we called him Santa Claus behind his back because of the way he looked, but this was the first time I saw how much he really cared. He was not eating anything himself, just nursing his drink and sitting in front of me, keeping an eye on my plate, serving me whatever I finished.

I was on my third piece of enchilada when I suddenly started crying. I didn't know what to do, so I just kept on chewing my enchilada through my tears, horribly embarrassed.

Mr Bose came and sat by my side, putting his arm around me comfortingly. None of the other diners could see us, since our table was in a corner, but the white-liveried waiter moved away discreetly, and I wondered what he must be thinking. The way the hostess had greeted him, Mr Bose seemed to be a regular at this expensive restaurant.

'I'm sorry,' I said, wiping my tears with my kurta sleeves. As usual, I wasn't carrying a handkerchief. Then I noticed the big fat white dupatta around my neck. Idiot.

'It's OK. It's good to cry sometimes, to let it all out,' he said quietly. Then, after a while, 'It's Karan, isn't it? Had a lover's tiff?'

I shook my head, looking down miserably at my plate. So even he knew. Of course he knew. I'd first met Karan when he was shooting an ad film for Mr Bose. It had never been a secret that we were going around. Why should I have expected that people wouldn't know that we'd broken up?

'You're taking all this very seriously right now, but in a couple of weeks, when you've kissed and made up, you'll even forget what you'd fought about in the first place,' he said, taking a sip of his screwdriver.

I didn't say anything, just covered my face with my hands and pressed my eyes. Even if Karan and I did ever make up, there was no way I could forget about the abortion, although sometimes I wondered whether it had actually happened at all. I hadn't even been able to believe that I was *pregnant,* in the first place, when I got the results from the lab...

I wiped my face with my dupatta and made myself look up at Mr Bose. I tried to think of some work-related stuff I could talk about with him. Nothing came to mind, so I just sat up straight, trying to appear composed. But he was looking at me so sympathetically, I had to bite my cheeks from inside to keep from starting to cry all over again.

'It's alright, baby.' He patted my arm reassuringly. 'Keeping it all bottled up won't help any.'

'I'm sorry...' I said. I was crying again. 'This is so dumb... I've become such a mess, I don't know...'

'Don't worry, everything will be alright soon,' he said comfortingly. 'Tiffs like this happen...'

'It's... it's not a tiff,' I told him. 'We didn't break up because of a fight. Karan called up one week after I had the... Karan called me up one day and told me point-blank that he doesn't want to be with me any longer.'

'Oh, lovers keep on saying things like that. Pyar mein ye sab to chalta rehta hai. Why, even now, when we have a fight, my wife declares that our marriage is over and storms off to her mother's place. I enjoy the peace and quiet in the house for a couple of days, then go and cajole and coax her into coming back. What's romance without a little bit of mirch-masala, huh?'

'No, no, it's not like that. It really *is* over. I didn't want to believe it either, when Karan told me. I kept on... calling him up, I even landed up at his place...'

I bit my lips, remembering that afternoon. Karan walking around the room, gesticulating, spewing out words that made barely any sense, as I sat on the sofa, too confused to even fight with him.

'It was just a physical affair for him,' I said dully, wiping my face. 'He said so himself. Clearly, directly. I'm the fool, I love... loved him so completely, I never even thought... I just kept on hoping... even after he told me ten times that it's over... that he'll understand that actually he loves me, he'll call up and tell me, "Paro, I made a big mistake, please forgive me, let's get married..." '"

I shut up, realising that I was talking like an idiot kid. But when I looked up at Mr Bose, I could see that he wasn't laughing at me. Even without being told about the abortion, he seemed to understand what I was going through. He offered me the screwdriver the waiter had kept in front of him. I hardly ever drank, but I sighed and picked it up, shrugging. I'd always liked orange juice.

I sipped it slowly, trying to look casual, then asked Mr Bose hesitantly, 'Is it possible for you to... talk to him...'

'I would have, but I don't think there is much point. Karan is not... the marrying type. At least not now, not for the next five-six years, I reckon,' Mr Bose said slowly, stroking his beard. 'Perhaps somebody should have... told you when you first got involved with him. Hadn't you had any affairs before?'

I shrugged. 'I come from a small town, so dating and all were out of the question... The only person I'd ever even had a major crush on was my graphic design teacher. For three years I attended all his lectures, sat on the first bench. Actually, most of the girls in my class used to freak out on him.' I gave a short laugh and shook my head. 'But he got married when we were in our final year. Beautiful wife he has. A Bengali.'

'Oh, you're quite beautiful, too. As a matter of fact, you even look a bit Bengali,' he said, trying to cheer me up. 'Where are you from?'

'Amravati,' I said, the mention of my hometown bringing a faint smile to my lips.

'What does your father do?'

'Papa passed away. When I was about seven.'

'Oh, I'm so sorry.'

I nodded.

'Ma works as a clerk in Bank of Maharashtra.'

We sipped our drinks in silence for a while.

'I don't know why I was so stupid, I even told Ma about Karan, when I first fell in love with him. She keeps on asking me – when are you getting married, shall I go and talk to his parents? I haven't told her that we've broken up, what if he wants to make up...' I massaged my forehead with my hand, then looked up at him. 'You must think I'm a fool, na, the way I'm going on?'

'I've been through this myself, I know what it feels like,' Mr Bose said gently. 'When I was in college, I was going around with this girl, Moloyshree – Molu, I used to call her. She was so beautiful, all these models, they're nothing in front of her. Sweet voice, too. She learnt Rabindra Sangeet because I like it. We were even planning to name our first son Rabindra.'

In spite of my depression, I wanted to smile, but didn't. Everybody in our office knew about Mr Bose's fascination with Tagore. He had felt very bad when Raghu had accidentally let it slip out that we called him Santa Claus. He'd thought that with his flowing white beard and longish hair, he looked like the poet.

'I tried so hard to convince her parents, but they wanted a boy who had a government job. A government job, can you imagine? I'm earning twenty times more than any government servant. It wasn't even as if we belonged to different castes. But they married her off to this boy – Alok Sarkar.' He spat out the name, as though it still tasted bad. 'I turned into a regular Devdas, let me tell you. I drank my way to hospital. My parents, my friends, they all tried to make me see reason, but nothing doing, I didn't care, I didn't want to live. You know how it feels.'

I nodded sympathetically. He finished his drink, and the waiter appeared with another. There was just a bit left in my glass, so I finished mine too, and the waiter put a fresh screwdriver in front of me. No harm in being a Devdas for one night, was there?

' "Jab dil hi toot gaya, hum jee ke kya karenge…" ' Mr Bose sang in a loud, off-key voice, trying to do Saigal's nasal twang. He looked at me and smiled. 'What comes after, come on, you're the one who's currently going through a heartbreak, you should know – "Maloom na tha itni mushkil…" '

I couldn't help smiling sheepishly as I admitted, 'I've been listening to "Tadap tadap ke is dil se…" '

'That one's good too, but "Jab dil hi toot gaya" is the classic. You must try crying to it sometime,' Mr Bose said, eyes twinkling. 'In my Devdas days, I used to go to music shops and say, "Give me sad songs – any film, any singer." I had the largest collection of heartbreak songs. Any friend of mine broke his heart, I was always willing to lend him some cassettes to cry over. Do you know that one – "Ye duniya gar chaman hoti, to barbadi ke veerane kahaan jaate…" '

I smiled and closed my eyes, leaning back in the soft leather seat. We were sitting in Mr Bose's BMW, which he'd parked in a small lane near Juhu beach. The rain had passed, leaving the air fresh and moist. I breathed deep, right down to my tummy. I was pleasantly drunk and the weight that had been pressing down on me seemed a bit lighter.

When I opened my eyes, I saw that Mr Bose was watching me with a smile. He took my hand in his and said softly, 'You won't believe me, it might not even seem possible now, Paro, but I'm older, I should know. There's one truth about heartbreaks – they heal with time.'

I shrugged, shaking my head. 'I don't know. Right now I'm feeling sho…' I caught myself slurring and laughed, embarrassed. 'I don't usually drink. I thought, why not be a Devdas for one day?'

'How can you be Devdas? You're Paro. The beautiful, arrogant Paro,' he said.

I sat up, wondering why he was calling me arrogant, then got what he was talking about. Devdas' Paro.

'You really are beautiful,' he said kindly. 'Haven't you ever thought of modelling?'

'Good God, no.'

'I'll shoot you sometime. You've got such lovely eyes. They're so warm, like a puppy's, no, like chocolate cake fresh out of the oven. Beautiful hair, too. You should leave it open more often.'

'It gets in my way while working.'

'Has anyone told you what gorgeous skin you have?' he continued. '"Wheatish" is such a dumb word. It's like almonds, no, like honey mixed with milk.'

'Karan used to say that my skin has got high reflectance,' I said.

'Oh, a cameraman's compliments!' he laughed. 'It's very soft as well, the camera can't see that.'

'"The secret is Silkina Moisturiser. 92.73% of the women who applied it twice a day reported soft, touch-me skin in just two weeks,"' I joked, quoting the ad we'd been making.

He touched my cheek with the back of his hand. 'You pass the soft, touch-me skin test with flying colours.'

It really was sweet of Mr Bose to try and boost my self-esteem this way, but my smile was starting to feel a bit strained. I told myself that I was being oversensitive, hyper, whatever. Mr Bose was old enough to be my father.

'What's happening with the Silkina Moisturiser ad? Did the client like it?' I asked.

'Routine stuff. They bounced it a couple of times, asked for some changes in the edit, and accepted it finally.'

'Sharmishtha was telling me that unless they do some kut-kut, the client's retenpratives – I mean re-pre-sen-tatives – feel that they're not earning their money.'

'That's part of the game. But let's forget about business for tonight. You know, Paro,' he said, his hand back on my cheek, 'life is too short to waste on tears.'

'I… uh… guess so.'

'Go out, enjoy yourself, Bombay's a great place to have fun.'

'"Be young, have fun, drink Pepsi."' There didn't seem to be any way I could remove his hand from my cheek without being terribly obvious about it. I tried awkwardly to change the topic. 'Have you done any commercials for a cola, sir?'

'Why are you still being so formal? "Sir" and all? After sharing our deepest secrets with each other? Hmmm?' His hand was playing with my hair now. 'I've always found you terribly attractive, Paro.'

I was too shocked to say anything for a moment. Then I stuttered out, 'But you're, like, married, no?'

'You're telling me? I wish I could forget about it for a single minute,' he said, laughing at his own joke. I laughed along weakly.

'But I don't… I mean, I'm still in love with Karan…' My cheeks were burning.

'You should forget Karan. Just get him out of your system. Here you are, crying over him, and he's been fucking around all over town.'

That couldn't be true, could it? Karan couldn't possibly be…

'"Take the cash and let the credit go…"' he said.

'I… I don't, but even if… You're so much older than me, sir. You're old enough to be my father.'

'Did you know that older men are much better in bed? They know how to really please a woman.'

Suddenly he leaned over and kissed me on the lips. I was too surprised and too drunk to react immediately, and before I knew what was happening, he was pushing his fat, pudgy hands down my kurta, sticking his tongue into my mouth. I tried to push him away, but he was too strong. All that food, I thought, a burst of hysterical laughter bubbling up inside me.

I twisted my face away from him. 'Please, Mr Bose, I don't...'

'Relax, Paro, why don't you just... allow yourself... relax and enjoy...'

He somehow managed to twist my face back and push his fat tongue into my mouth again. I could feel his erection grinding into my thigh, his tongue wriggling in my mouth like a fish. I wanted to throw up. My right arm was pinned by my side because of his weight. With my left hand I tried to push him off, but I just couldn't. I closed my eyes tight and tried to blot out what was happening. It was someone else whose nipples he was pinching, someone else whose thighs he was trying to push apart...

Mr Bose drew back when he realised that I was crying. I held my kurta together with shaking hands and tried to cover myself up with my dupatta. My bra had come undone and I didn't know how to do it up with him sitting by my side.

'Don't cry, please don't cry,' he said awkwardly.

I kept on crying, partly because I couldn't stop, and partly because I wanted him to feel guilty. Actually, no. I shouldn't have cared enough about the bastard even to want to make him feel guilty. Who cared? Did that make any sense? Did anything make much sense any more?

He kept on asking me the way home and I gave him a few short instructions, here and there. I didn't want to co-operate with him one bit, not even to help him find the way to my place. Actually, it may have been because I was too drunk. Or maybe because I was crying too hard.

'You've turned into a crying jag,' he said, patting my hand. I drew it back immediately. 'Happens to the best of us sometimes.'

I howled into my dupatta, refusing to look at him. He cleared his throat. Of course. He wanted me to get out. I fumbled with the stupid newfangled door handle and stumbled out.

He leaned over and closed the door, looking up at me through the window.

'You're overreacting, Paro,' he told me with his usual air of benevolent authority. 'You were probably too upset to start off with, about Karan and all. And of course, you're not used to the booze. Anyway, now you just hop into bed and sleep it off. See you in the office on Monday.'

I couldn't think of a single thing to say, just stood there watching him as he started the car and sped off into the dark.

The landlady and her husband stared at me as I passed them on the stairs, clutching the dupatta to my face. Fuck them. Who cared?

I scrubbed and scrubbed, trying to wash the imprint of his hands off my skin. Suddenly, I felt a wave of nausea come up and I puked it all out into the bathroom sink – the remnants of the enchiladas, the brownish-orange orange juice, hopefully all the vodka, too.

I washed my face and looked into the mirror above the sink. My lips were swollen, my eyes were bloodshot. In a strange kind of way, I looked... sexy. I wanted to take a blade and slash my face. Even my hair looked dishevelled, wild, the way it did when Karan and I had just made love. He would lie on the bed, watching me as I combed my hair…

I picked up the scissors that were lying in front of the mirror and tried to hack my hair but it just got caught between the blades. I pulled the scissors away, wincing as my hair got plucked, and threw them on the bathroom floor angrily. Even the bloody fucking scissors had to be blunt!

Clutching a towel around me, I swayed into the room, and crashed out on the bed, too tired to change into my nighty, too tired to switch off the light, too tired to put on the fan.

First day in Bombay. Welcome back to Bombay!

TWO

'Of course, I have to resign tomorrow,' I said.

'Why? Why should *you* resign? You should sue the bastard, drag him into court for sexual harassment,' Saira said. 'There was this Supreme Court judgement...'

'A court case?' I laughed humourlessly. 'Are you mad? I'll be forty-five by the time it gets settled. OK, he jumped on my bones, but what do I say in court? That I went out for dinner with him, cried on his shoulder about my heartbreak, got drunk of my own free will, and it's sexual harassment because he's my boss and makes a pass at me? Huh!'

Saira bit into her green salad furiously. Firstly, she was angry, and secondly, her salad did require a lot of chewing. I slathered some more butter on my pav bhaji. Who the hell wanted to have a 'good figure' any more? Eat food fit for cows and buffaloes, endure the pangs of hunger same as a person below the poverty line, and feel very proud of my self-control? For whom?

'All men are bastards,' Kavita said quietly.

Saira and I nodded our heads in agreement. If there was one thing that all of us had discovered since coming to Bombay, it was this axiom. I had been the last one to catch on.

When I was going around with Karan, I was sitting on cloud nine, looking at the world through rose-tinted glasses, telling my friends that they had let themselves get too bitter and cynical. When I fell down, back onto reality, they were kind enough to keep their 'I-told-you-so's to themselves.

'I can't believe that I was so, so dumb. I should've realised that Mr Bose was being so kind and sympathetic and all just because... just because he wanted to fuck me.' I could feel the anger come up like bile in my throat. 'I should've *known* as soon as he mentioned the word "dinner". But I was this bloody nitwit, thinking he's a nice guy because he's so intellectual and well-read and artistic.'

'How can somebody who loves Tagore be such a scumbag?' Kavita said.

'I wish I had his residence number,' I said. 'I'd call up his wife and tell her what a lech her husband is.'

'Married men are the worst,' Kavita said.

'You can find out his residence number from your office,' Saira suggested, always practical.

'I don't feel like going back to office.'

'Why? Hey man, to hell with your boss,' Saira said impatiently. 'You just go and start working in the office from Monday, Paro. If *he* kicks you out, we'll see to him.'

'I don't know, but meeting him again...' I remembered his hands on my breasts and felt like squirming. 'I'd feel kind of... humiliated.'

'Why the hell should *you* feel humiliated?' Saira argued. '*He's* the one who's been a jerk.'

'Ya, but he's seen me like that – almost topless – don't you understand?' I even had a love bite above my left breast. A love bite, for Chrissake!

Saira started to say something more, but Kavita touched her arm, so she shut up. Kavita was the oldest amongst the three of us – twenty-seven. She was quiet and straightforward, no frills to the way she spoke, or the way she dressed. I'd never seen her in anything except jeans and plain T-shirts. Saira always wore sarees. Not that she was traditional, far from it. She just felt that they hid her fat better. She worked as a journalist for a daily newspaper and one would've thought that she'd be more comfortable getting around in jeans. But she claimed that she could even climb a tree in a saree.

'One mango milkshake,' I said to the wizened old waiter and tried to smile back at him, swallowing the lump in my throat. The nicest thing about this Udupi restaurant was the waiters – they didn't mind us sitting and chatting for hours as long as at least one of us was eating or drinking something.

'One chocolate milkshake for me,' Kavita told him, inspired.

'"Chocolate cake,"' I said, shaking my head. 'Actually, Mr Bose kept on comparing me with things to eat. Probably can't think very far beyond food. No wonder he's so fat. Eyes like chocolate cake – can you imagine? Milk and honey skin!' I was trying to joke, but nobody found it very funny.

'You should've told him to take his chocolate cake and stuff it up his ass,' Saira said.

'This morning I was thinking, when Mr Bose said to me, "I wish I could forget that I'm married," I should've said, "It's obvious that you don't let your marital status stop you from playing around. But I..." No, that's too long, I should just have told him that I'm not interested. Period. And before leaving, when he said, "You're overreacting, Paro," I should've said...'

Kavita touched my hand gently. I drew it back. I didn't want her sympathy. It made me feel like crying. Anger felt much better, it felt strong. It made me feel like getting up and fighting, not just lying on in the dust, weeping.

'I don't know what the hell I was doing crying in front of him about Karan. I didn't even let myself cry in front of Ma when I went home, because she would have got upset... and you know how mothers are, she would have got it out of me about the abortion. I was so irritable all the time, I kept on snapping at her. She thought that it was because I'd been dieting, so she kept on feeding me and I kept on puking it all up. It was so bloody ridiculous...'

'You must've needed the relief after holding yourself back for so long,' Kavita said.

'So I could have gone and cried into my pillow,' I said. 'I've been making such a fool of myself – crying in front of my boss... and oh God, I don't even know who all saw me crying that day on that Silkina moisturiser shoot.'

'Why don't you join another production house, Paro?' Kavita suggested.

'Ya, I could do that... But it's not easy, getting work. I had to job-hunt for more than three months after I came to Bombay. Of course, I have six months of experience now... But anyway... even if I do get a job elsewhere...'

'Anyway what?'

'Well, Karan's a cameraman, he can shoot ads for any production house. If I meet him again... It was so humiliating that day, when we were shooting that Silkina Moisturiser ad, I didn't quite beg Karan, but he wasn't speaking to me and I... Shit, man, forget about it. Anyway, I can hardly say to my new employers, can I, "I'm not going to work for you if you use this cameraman"?'

'What are you going to do, then? Run away, back to your hometown?' Saira asked.

I had thought about it, but it had been so much of a struggle to leave Amravati in the first place. None of the girls in my group had believed me when I'd said that I would go to Bombay and become a set designer some day. I'd had to work so hard for it – getting the best marks in my commercial art class, saving up my scholarship money, convincing my mother to let me go. I was the youngest in the family, so I'd always been her baby. She had her misgivings, but she'd put them aside because she wanted the best for me. She wanted me to have all the opportunities she hadn't had. She wanted me to soar. If I chucked up my career and went back home, what would she...

'Hey, I've got an idea,' Kavita said suddenly. 'A friend of mine was working as an assistant director on a Hindi film. He quit a couple of days back. I don't know if assisting on films is the same as working on ads, but if you're interested...'

'... and the hero discovers that the heroine's father is the one who has murdered his father when he was a child. He goes to kill her father, dressed in full black, hair gelled back, carrying a three nought three rifle in his hands, riding bareback on a black horse. We see him in long shot as the horse jumps over the gates of her mansion. And then – khachack – zoom in to tight close shot of his eyes. Cut. Same shot repeat. Zoom. Cut. Zoom. Cut. Zoom. Cut.' Jambuwant Sinha looked at me proudly.

I nodded. I was not unmindful of the honour the director was bestowing upon me by giving me a complete narration of the script, including dialogues spoken with full emotion. He was describing the shot breakdown at important points, even providing sound effects at dramatic moments. I was trying hard to look interested, but my eyes kept on getting glazed over.

'He shouts, "Come on out, Thakur, your death is standing here, waiting for you. The curtain has now risen..." Manoj, check whether that chutiya Munshi has written the dialogues for tomorrow's shoot. Yes, so the hero says, "The curtain has now risen on your black deeds. You assumed..."'

Manoj, his chief assistant director, passed him his mobile phone. 'Munshi,' Manoj whispered.

'Yes, Munshiji. So, everything fine? Good, good...' Mr Sinha got up, spat out a gob of red betel juice from the window, and stood there, scratching his neck as he discussed the dialogues. He was short and dark and very fat, but he seemed to be absolutely comfortable in his own skin. The top three buttons of his yellow silk kurta were open, proudly exposing two thick gold chains resting on a mat of curly black hair.

A boy served me a brownish-green sherbet in a glass which had XXX Rum written on it. I took a sip, then two. I couldn't make out the flavour, but I was glad for the break. Mr Sinha's office was like nothing I had ever seen before. Forget about tables, there weren't even any chairs. The seating was Indian-style, if you could call it that. A huge mattress with an orange velvet sheet on it covered more than half the room. The room itself must have been a bright orange colour once upon a time. The paint was faded and chipped and worn away to reveal the green underneath. Especially near the mattress where people had leant on the walls instead of the purple heart-shaped cushions that were scattered around.

The only chakachak thing in the room was the huge framed poster of *Ghayal Parinda* – Jambuwant Sinha's last film and most major success to date. Mehboob Khan stared out of the poster at me, blood dripping from his nose and lips, a rifle, probably a three nought three, in his hands. An assortment of villains graced the centre, while a heroine, whom I couldn't recognise, posed on the other side, biting the edge of her dupatta coyly as she gazed at Mehboob Khan. The dupatta did nothing to cover the rest of her, however. Masses of boobs spilled out from her low-cut choli. In case one missed the point, there were two spirals of sequins on the choli, culminating in mirrors over the nipples.

I wanted to get up and make a dash for it. But I'd already submitted my resignation at Mr Bose's office. Since I hadn't given any notice, I hadn't got my pay for the last month. My landlady would expect her two thousand rupees on the first, or it was out on the streets for me unless I could...

'Munshi will meet me at Juhu Centaur in forty-five minutes,' Mr Sinha said. 'Manoj, call the car. What's your name... Chandramukhi, Manoj will tell you the rest of the script later.'

I nodded, trying not to look too glad.

'Manoj, tell her how to get to the set. She'll be handling costumes and continuity.'

'I'd rather be handling the set and props, sir,' I put in quickly as I struggled to my feet. 'I've done my graduation in commercial art, and I want to become an art director, so...'

'No problem. You can work on the set also. Everybody does everything here. Feel free, feel free...'

And he was gone.

It was past midnight, but there was no question of sleep – Iron Maiden was going great guns in our room, at full volume, with the treble turned high, so that every clang and high-pitched whine came through and cut to the bone. I lay on my side of the bed, hands crossed over my chest, staring at the ceiling fan, determined not to phone Karan.

There was no point in humiliating myself any further, but I desperately wanted to call him up and tell him what had happened with Mr Bose. Maybe he'd get angry and go and bash him up. Angry about what, though? About wanting to fuck me? That's all Karan had wanted too, he'd said so himself, that day at his place. But maybe he'd said it, and said it so crudely at that, just so as to make it clear to me that it really was over. He must have felt overwhelmed by the news that I was pregnant. We'd been going around for only four months. As it is, all the magazines said that men were commitment-shy.

Even I hadn't thought about the future – just being in love was enough. The last thing I'd wanted was to get pregnant. That day, when I'd walked into the lab to pick up my pregnancy report, I'd been praying that it was negative. But in my heart of hearts, I knew that I was worrying unnecessarily. I was a hypochondriac and all my fears always proved to be unfounded. I took the envelope from the clerk and opened it. I just couldn't believe my eyes – Pregnancy Test: Positive.

'Oh my God, oh my God,' I kept on whispering, again and again, till it registered that the clerk was staring at me. I hurried out and broke into a run. Karan's apartment was just ten minutes from the lab and I was halfway there, when I remembered Geetamaushi admonishing my sister that Moms-to-be are not supposed to run. I slowed down and placed a cautious hand on my tummy. God, Mom-to-be! This was crazy, man, this was surreal.

I rang the doorbell and counted to ten before pressing it again, harder. Karan opened the door with a jerk, scowling. Then he saw me and his sleepy face broke into a huge grin. I bounded into his arms and kissed him passionately.

'I must have got out of bed the right side today,' he said, running his hands down my back. 'Talking of beds...'

'Uh, I've got to tell you something,' I said, holding back.

'Hmm?' he said, ruffling my hair. 'You're looking very intense. What is it?'

I bit my lips, then blurted out, 'I'm pregnant.'

I waited, holding my breath, waited for him to say something. He rubbed his stubble and moved back. I crossed my arms tightly, trying to stop the trembling that had suddenly come up. He opened the curtains on the window, letting in the morning light.

'I need to brush my teeth,' he said.

Karan took a sip of the black tea I'd made for him and nodded. 'It's just right,' he said.

I watched him take another sip. He probably needed some time to get used to the idea, I told myself.

'Karan...' I said.

'Look, Paro, I don't know how we're going to manage this,' he said, keeping the teacup on a side-table. 'I'm just breaking into the big league right now. I have to concentrate on my work. So do you.'

'Ya, I suppose so,' I said a little uncertainly. 'I don't know how I'm going to balance my work and having a baby, of all the things in the world. Maybe I can do some graphic design work on a computer at home, but obviously it doesn't compare with working in a production house...'

'You should have an abortion,' he said.

'Karan, we can't... Not an abortion,' I said, holding his hand. 'We should have been more careful, and I'm sure that it's going to be a bit of a pain in the neck... But God, imagine, Karan, a *baby*! I know everybody has babies, but it's like a miracle, na?'

'What's the point of bringing an unwanted child into the world?' Karan said, leaning back and looking at me.

I backtracked, told him that I didn't mind making the sacrifice, he could continue concentrating on his career, I could always start working after the baby went to school, we'd be so happy together... It took quite a while for it to sink in that he really didn't want the baby, that basically, he didn't want to marry me.

I cried, I pleaded, I made him put his hand on my tummy, I even got hysterical – but nothing worked. He was firm and quiet. He had not made a commitment. He would not marry me for the sake of the baby. An abortion was the only choice.

We went to a doctor that afternoon, and by next morning, it was all over. I didn't mind the pain and the bleeding. It seemed right, somehow, that it should hurt. I didn't go to work, didn't bother to eat much, didn't do anything except sit in my room and cry. In the days that followed, I needed Karan desperately, but he had gone out of town for a shoot and I couldn't get through to his mobile.

The doctor had given me some tablets for the pain, and I started eating twice the prescribed dosage because they made me feel drowsy. But I couldn't forget even in my sleep, I just kept on having nightmares...

'Fly, fly to the sun...' Iron Maiden boomed away, completely out of sync with my feelings. I told myself firmly that I needed to stop thinking about the abortion and get some sleep. Tomorrow was to be my first day of work with Mr Sinha. Thinking about it wasn't going to change what had happened. But my head kept running around in circles, trying to understand what had happened, to make sense of it all.

Maybe I could have had the baby by myself... But how would I have managed? I couldn't have had the baby and continued to work in Bombay. I would have had to go back home. Ma would've been aghast. I had never even heard of an unwed mother in Amravati. OK, so they would've shouted at me and maybe even hit me, and worst of all, Ma would've been heartbroken that she'd failed to bring up her daughter properly. But they wouldn't have chucked me out of the house.

I could have taken up a job after the baby was about six months old. I would've had to keep it in a crèche when I went out to work... How would people have reacted to the whole thing? I could have dealt with the disapproval, but what about the baby? There was a girl in my school whose parents were divorced. Our classmates used to tease her mercilessly. Some of them were even told by their parents not to talk to her – it could be a bad influence.

It wouldn't have been easy for my child to grow up in Amravati with the stigma of illegitimacy. I wouldn't have been able to give it a very good life, but surely any kind of life was better than none at all. It must have been so happy inside me, free-floating in the fluid, feeling warm and safe, never imagining that a steel instrument would come and rip it out...

'It was *not* a baby,' Karan had shouted at me when I'd started getting hysterical about how we'd killed our baby.

'There was a possibility that it would have grown into a baby, but it was just a foetus, that's all.'

I'd asked the doctor how big it was and she'd said that it was about an inch long. It hadn't been a baby, but it would have become one, if only Karan had also wanted it to. If only Karan had loved me enough to marry me.

Was it really possible that Karan had not loved me at all? OK, he hadn't, as he said, ever made an outright commitment. Maybe I'd just assumed, with my small-town sensibilities, that when you fell in love, you got married. But what about all those emails he'd sent me whenever he went for outdoor shoots? Especially that one in which he'd written, 'I didn't know how lost I was till I found you. I'm never going to let you go.' And what about when I'd cried in his arms after we first made love? He'd kissed away my tears, telling me that he loved me, he'd always love me. And I'd told him I was crying because I was feeling so happy, so beautiful. I'd been a half and he made me whole... God, what a dumb metaphor! Everything seemed dumb now, everything seemed ugly. I turned away from Shweta so that she couldn't see me crying.

After a while, I got up to get a glass of water. On my way to the kitchen, I passed through the dark living room and somehow, I found myself by the phone, my fingers jabbing out the familiar number.

I listened to the ring, heart thudding, imagining the phone ringing in his mood-lit apartment. He'd turn down the volume on the TV, curse when he saw that the cordless phone wasn't near him, struggle to get off the beanbag, walk across to the...

'Hello!' Karan said.

I was hearing his voice after almost three weeks.

'Hello,' he said, a little louder. 'Hello, who is it? Hello?'

I sat down on the floor, feeling sick to my stomach. Suddenly, I realised that he might guess from the sound of Iron Maiden in the background that it was me on the line. I quickly put the receiver back on the cradle.

'Oh, shit!' I said softly. But then, what if he did guess that it was me? What was the worst that could happen? Maybe he'd call me back. I laughed at myself and shook my head.

Why did I have to be so stupid?

THREE

The first day of the shooting schedule started off with a minor disaster – the hero, Mehboob Khan, arrived on time. He was supposed to be present on the set by 8:30 a.m., but nobody even remotely expected him to be punctual. In the previous schedule, he'd never once made an entrance before lunchtime for a 9:00 a.m. shift.

Before he arrived, the set was looking like the quiet little hill station it was supposed to be. A couple of light-boys were peacefully unloading lights from a truck. The art director's team was digging holes by the sides of the freshly-tarred roads and planting pine trees, roots and all. Manoj, the chief assistant director, was showing me around the set as we ate wada-pavs.

It was the first time I was seeing such a big outdoor set and I explored it enthusiastically. Constructed on a hilltop in Film City, the set was a picture-book depiction of a hill station, with façades of slate-roofed cottages, and winding roads that criss-crossed each other at will. A quaint red-bricked church overlooked the chowk which formed the nucleus of the hill station. Shops selling handicrafts and well-off residential houses lined the streets that sloped away from it. A modern touch was added by the Tehelka Barber Shop. Inside it was the production manager's office, where he was sleeping with his feet on the table. Manoj hid one of his shoes behind a tin trunk and put a finger on his lips as we tiptoed out of the office.

'He's the producer's brother-in-law,' Manoj told me, grinning.

I didn't want to get involved in any politics, but Manoj's glee was so contagious, I started to smile.

'Don't think that he doesn't deserve it,' he said. 'He's eaten so much money in the construction of this set, it would have been cheaper to shoot outdoors, on location.'

'Will we be going outdoors for any shoot?' I asked.

'We've finished all the location shoots, thank God,' he told me as we walked down a meandering street. 'The rest of the film will be shot here.'

'The set looks really good because it's not built on flat land,' I said. 'The ups and downs will give a picturesque look to the film.'

'Ya, but we're going to get jacked taking track shots,' Manoj said. 'The art director's happily...'

A loud honk made us jump. We turned in time to see a black and silver Pajero zoom past and brake further down the road. Manoj ran off towards it, then ran back, shoved his half-eaten wada-pav into my hand and ran back again. I saw the tracks that had been made by the Pajero on the freshly-tarred road and thought that Manoj had gone to fire the driver – when I saw Mehboob Khan step out.

I followed Manoj and hovered around, hiding our wada-pavs behind my back, wondering whether I was going to be introduced. I wasn't.

I stared at Mehboob Khan as Manoj settled him into a chair and served him tea in an elegant bone china cup that had appeared from nowhere. His face was so familiar, it was a shock to realise that I was actually seeing him for just the first time. My cousins, Sharada and Savita, had his posters plastered all over their bedroom walls. They'd be squealing with delight if they knew I was standing just ten feet away from him.

He was a big man, over six feet tall. The hand that held the delicate china cup was huge and looked even more imposing with the two diamond rings sparkling on his fingers. Somehow, everything about him seemed exaggerated, larger than life – the kajal-lined glittering eyes, the heavy jaw and full lips, even the mane of obviously-coloured light brown hair that brushed his shoulders. He was wearing knee-high laced-up leather boots and tight jeans that lovingly showed all the hours he'd spent at the gym. The translucent golden shirt that was open to mid-chest would have looked ridiculous on a lesser man, but on Mehboob Khan, it looked just right.

'Go and call Jumbo on his mobile. Tell him that Mehboob Khan is here,' Manoj whispered furiously to me.

'Jumbo…?' I said.

'Jumbo, Jumboji!' Manoj clapped his head with his hand. 'Jambuwant Sinha. Run.'

I ran. But I didn't know where I was running. Everybody else on the set seemed to be running around too and nobody had the time to tell me from where I could make a call.

'Just a second, this is important...' I said to a man who was carrying a ladder.

'Get out of the way,' he screamed at me.

'I... Aaah!' I shrieked as a big pine tree crashed down six feet from where I was standing.

'What... what...' For a moment I didn't know what to do, then got my wits together and retreated into the shelter of a verandah, not that it made any difference now. The art director's team hurriedly picked up the tree and set about planting it again.

A car door slammed loudly. I peeped out to see Jambuwant Sinha get out of a red Mercedes. His pot belly wobbled as he half-walked, half-ran towards Mehboob Khan.

'Mehboob! I can't tell you how happy I am to see you again!' Mr Sinha cried out, embracing the star like a long-lost brother. 'How nice of you to come! And so early in the morning!'

In a jiffy, the camera was set up on a crane and the market lane near the chowk was lit with HMI lights and huge satin cloths that fluttered in the wind, threatening to topple over. Everybody was working frantically, especially the art director's team which seemed to have gone crazy, slapping bright yellow paint on the railings around the chowk and planting pine trees on every empty space they could find.

Manoj was running towards Mr Sinha when he saw me and thrust a big notepad into my hands.

'Manoj, Manoj!' I ran with him. 'What am I supposed to do with this?'

'Haven't you written continuity before?' he said, stopping.

'No,' I said, feeling especially inept.

He flicked the notepad open impatiently and pointed to the printed columns. 'You write down the scene number, the shot number, the take number, whether it's OK or N.G. and a description of everything that happens in each take. Got it?'

Mehboob Khan strode into the market lane, wearing a red kurta over an orange dhoti and white Rajasthani mojris. His spot boy, who was much shorter than him, ran behind, trying to keep his head covered with a dark blue umbrella.

'Everything,' I said, looking at Manoj's back as he ran towards Mr Sinha.

'Give me the dialogues,' Mehboob Khan said impatiently, checking his reflection in the lens of the camera.

Manoj tapped Mr Sinha's shoulder and whispered something in his ear. Mr Sinha stared at Manoj for a minute, then turned slowly to Mehboob Khan and cleared his throat. 'You look really handsome in red – really handsome. Like a red flower blooming in the desert.'

'You're not looking bad yourself. You've lost weight, haan?' Mehboob Khan said genially, patting Mr Sinha's paunch. 'You're not dieting, are you?'

'If I diet, who'll take you as the hero?' Mr Sinha grinned.

Mehboob Khan put an arm around Mr Sinha's shoulders and said, 'Don't lose too much weight, my jaan, otherwise you'll disappear.'

Mr Sinha laughed like it was the funniest joke he had ever heard. He was a good six inches shorter than Mehboob and even with the alleged weight-loss, more than twice as broad. Everybody around the camera laughed along obediently. I tried to laugh, and all that came out was a miserable titter. I'd have made a lousy actress.

'Enough joking-voking,' the star declared suddenly. 'I'm full power today. Let's shoot.'

He took one look at the sheet of dialogues Manoj showed him, and nodded dismissively.

'He gets the dialogues really fast,' Kapil, the other assistant director, whispered to me. I nodded, not looking at him, because I was watching the rehearsal intently. I didn't want to miss a thing.

'Action!' Mr Sinha called out.

'Get out of my way, you dog,' Mehboob Khan shouted at the junior artiste who cowered in front of him. The camera craned down to capture the hero's expression of disdain.

'Very good. Marvellous,' Mr Sinha cried out. 'But a little more of... of hurt. You are a quiet man, a peaceful man, a lion who would never have attacked anybody if he had not been wounded. You know, you know what I mean. I know you can do it. Action!'

Mehboob Khan did one rehearsal after another, but Mr Sinha kept on asking for 'one more rehearsal, please.' The emotion was just a little off or the emphasis was on the wrong word or...

'Enough!' Mehboob Khan shouted. 'You just take the bloody shot now.'

'Mehboob-jaan.' Mr Sinha walked up and put an arm around the star's shoulders. 'There's been a slight problem.'

'What problem,' Mehboob said impatiently.

'Just two minutes more,' Jambuwant Sinha said soothingly. 'It'll come soon, don't worry.'

'What'll come?' Mehboob said, confused. 'I'm telling you, the emotion is fine.'

'No, no, not the emotion,' Mr Sinha said, patting his arm. 'The raw stock. The production manager's gone to get the negative film. On a motorcycle. He called me right now from Film City gate. He'll be here before you can...'

Mehboob roared and threw off Mr Sinha's arm.

'You fucking idiots don't know how to utilise Mehboob Khan's time,' the star declared regally. 'You don't deserve his time. Pack Up!'

And he walked off. Manoj ran behind, begging him not to leave. Mehboob Khan stopped just once and what followed was ten minutes of the star questioning the parentage and virtue of various female relatives of Manoj, the production manager and even Mr Sinha. Manoj's face tightened, but he continued apologising to Mehboob Khan till the star got into his Pajero and drove off in a roar of exhaust.

It was Mr Sinha's turn now to throw every ma-bahen ki gaali I'd heard, and more, at Mehboob Khan. I shifted uncomfortably. Mr Bose was always cool and in control on the sets. It wasn't as if he never swore, but he had so much class, four-letter words didn't seem dirty coming from him. Which should teach me not to go by appearances.

'Eight years ago, when *I* gave him a break, Mehboob was ready to lick my shoes. Just because he's had some hits, he thinks he can behave any bloody way he likes with me? "Pack Up!" he declares! On *my* set! I'll kick that bastard out of my film, I'll show him…' Mr Sinha threatened unconvincingly.

The assistant art director, who was standing near me, sniggered, but shut up when Manoj shot a warning look at him. It took about five more minutes for Mr Sinha to blow off all his steam, after which he slumped tiredly into a chair.

'Hey, somebody get me some chai,' Mr Sinha said. He wiped his face and called Munshiji, the scriptwriter. Since the props and the lights had been set up in the market, he told Munshiji to write a scene for Rahul Kapoor and Mrignayani set in the market.

In the commotion following Mehboob Khan's arrival, I hadn't even noticed the presence of the other actors on the set. Although Mrignayani was a newcomer, nobody had to tell me that she was the heroine. I'd heard the phrase 'hourglass figure' n number of times before, but I really understood what it means when I saw her. She had the tiniest waist I'd ever seen, huge hips and a bosom that bounced happily when she walked. She was quite attractive above the neck as well – milky white skin (no question of honey here), full red lips and big kajal-lined eyes that sparkled flirtatiously as she chatted with the cameraman.

Munshiji, the scriptwriter, sat down on a chair near Mr Sinha, put on his thick reading glasses, opened his dog-eared notebook, uncapped his fountain pen, and stared at the blank page intently for a good ten minutes.

'We can put in this scene after Mehboob Khan meets Rahul Kapoor for the first time,' Mr Sinha said helpfully, taking a bit of lime on his finger and touching it lightly to his tongue. He'd opened a silver box of betel leaves on his lap and was making paan for himself. The process seemed to be having a therapeutic effect on him.

'Yes, but what will *happen* in the scene?' Munshiji asked sadly. As it is, he was a small, frail-looking old man, and with this additional burden on him, he looked ready to break down.

Manoj gestured to me. I got up and followed him as he weaved his way through half a dozen huge sheets of satin stretched out on stands. He'd stuffed his hands into his pockets and didn't look at me till we reached the post office around the corner. I was wondering whether he was feeling depressed after the firing Mehboob Khan had given him, but he smiled cheerfully as he held the big wooden door open for me.

'Your Highness, your kingdom awaits you,' he said with a bow.

I felt like I'd stepped into Alladin's cave. The room was filled with silk, chiffon and satin costumes of the brightest hues imaginable. The colours were so dazzling, they almost hurt the eye – parrot green, electric blue, blood red, fluorescent orange.

It took me a moment to realise that there was a method to this madness. The costumes were hung in two rows along the walls and one row running down the middle of the room. Big tin trunks with the actors' names painted on them in crude white letters were lined below the costumes. One of the trunks had Mehboob Khan written on it, with the 'Meh' scratched out. Maybe Manoj was less equanimous than he looked.

'Here are your dress-men,' Manoj said, gesturing towards the two men who were ironing costumes on a long wooden table by the side of the door. One of them smiled sweetly at me. I smiled back, trying to remember where I had met him before.

'That's Bihari and that's Take Two,' Manoj said.

I nodded, then asked the familiar-looking man, 'Your name is Tekattu?'

'Take Two,' Manoj laughed.

I looked at him uncomprehendingly.

'When we're shooting, the first time we take a shot, it's called Take One. If the first take is not OK, we have to re-shoot, and the second time, we call it Take Two and so on,' he explained.

'Ya, ya, I know that. I've worked on ads,' I said.

'So this guy, he's Keshto Mukherjee, Take Two. Just Take Two for short.'

'Oh, like that.' No wonder I'd thought that I knew him. He was a carbon copy of the sixties' comedian, with his rolling eyes and lopsided grin. He even looked like the first thing he'd done in the morning was down a peg of whisky and was very happy for the effort.

I realised that Manoj hadn't told them my name, so I introduced myself. Take Two nodded at me, then looked away and shuffled his feet. Bihari, who was stout and hairy and a little scary-looking in the bargain, nodded seriously.

Manoj opened one of the tin trunks that were lined below the rows of costumes. He took out two heavy albums, and pushing the costumes back, sat on another tin trunk. Since there were no chairs, I also sat on the edge of a tin trunk, bending forward to avoid touching the costumes that were hanging over it.

'Sit comfortably, yaar, relax,' Manoj said, pushing back the costumes above my head. He opened an album and showed me a still photograph of Mehboob Khan, dressed in a black vest and bright yellow pants, ladaoing panja with Rahul Kapoor, who was wearing a silver-coloured shirt and shocking pink pants.

'Rahul Kapoor's costume has to be the same as this one. Mrignayani wasn't there in the previous scene, so she has to be given a new set of clothes. For the continuity costumes, you just have to give the continuity still to the dress-men and double-check the costumes they bring out,' he explained to me and then told the dress-men to take out Rahul Kapoor's continuity clothes and Mrignayani's red ghagra-choli.

I was flicking through the album of still photographs when Mrignayani bounced into the Costume Room. 'I'll choose my own clothes, I'll choose my own clothes,' she cried out in a little-girl voice.

'Just for today,' Manoj grumbled, but his eyes followed her appreciatively as she walked down the aisle and disappeared behind a row of costumes.

'Manoj,' I asked, 'in some stills Mrignayani wears city-girl clothes – jeans and miniskirts and short tops – and in other stills she's a typical village girl. Does she have a double role?'

'No, no,' he said, laughing. 'She looks good in both get-ups, so we make her wear whatever we feel like.'

'But where is she supposed to be from?'

'She belongs to this place, this hill station, Ramgarh. Her father's the richest man here. He starts off as a milkman, but Destiny shines on him and he wins a lottery ticket. He sends her to college, in the city, so she wears all these miniskirts. But she's a simple girl at heart. Her father's forgotten about his roots, about his cows and buffaloes. But she hasn't. She still loves them. That's why she even milks the cows.'

'Everyday?'

He stared at me. 'No, not everyday. Only once in the film, as a matter of fact. That's enough to establish it. The milking scene will get a lot of claps in the B-centres. Especially in the cow-belt, in Uttar Pradesh and Bihar. If you want to make proper masala Hindi films, you have to know how audiences react in the cow-belt. You want to make Hindi films?'

'Uh? No, I don't,' I said. 'Are you from… the cow-belt?'

'No, no. Jumbo is from Bihar. That's why he's got his finger on the pulse of the masses. I'm from right here. South Bombay, in fact. I studied at St. Xavier's College. But I went to Bihar, stayed there for one whole month and watched four films a day in the theatres,' Manoj said, looking very proud of himself.

'His father is a beeeg film distributor,' Mrignayani said, peeking out from behind the costumes just above Manoj's head. 'He won't have any problems getting finance for his first film. You'll take me in your film, won't you?'

'Ya, sure, I'll take you,' Manoj grinned, bending back to look at her.

Mrignayani pulled his hair playfully and told me, 'I even have a song in which Rahul Kapoor and me are riding on a buffalo. One buffalo.'

'That must be... interesting,' I said, for want of a better thing to say. 'But I thought that you're supposed to be Mehboob Khan's girlfriend in the film?'

'See, it's a very simple story,' Manoj said, trying to make Mrignayani massage his back, but she twisted his ear and flounced off. 'Till what point did Jumbo tell you the script?'

'Till Mehboob Khan goes to Mrignayani's father's mansion and shouts, "Your death is..."'

'Correct,' Manoj said, putting his feet on another costume trunk and making himself comfortable. 'Mrignayani's father comes out. Mehboob Khan aims his rifle and presses the trigger. But Mrignayani's father doesn't die. Why?'

'Why?' I asked.

'Because Mehboob Khan's mother comes in between. She gets shot and as she's dying in his arms, she makes him swear that he won't kill Mrignayani's father.'

'Why does she do that?'

'*That* is the secret. Which we'll reveal only in the climax. Anyway, Mrignayani's father tells her that Mehboob Khan is a goonda, madman, etc., etc. She still loves Mehboob, but he ignores her totally. So she starts flirting with Rahul Kapoor who has come to this hill station from the city for a holiday. She thinks Mehboob will get jealous, but instead, the two heroes become great friends.'

'Does Rahul Kapoor fall in love with Mrignayani?'

'Uh… Yes, yes, of course he does. After some three-four songs, he's even going to marry her. But in the end, he doesn't. He sacrifices his love and lets her marry Mehboob Khan.'

'Because he realises that she loves Mehboob Khan?' I said.

'No. Because he finds out that Mehboob Khan's father was actually his father.'

'So he and Mehboob Khan are brothers?'

'No,' Manoj said proudly. 'Mrignayani's father is actually Mehboob Khan's father, not Mrignayani's father. *That's why* Mehboob Khan's mother has not let him kill Mrignayani's father, means, his *real* father.'

'Oh,' I said, trying to figure that out. 'Oh.'

'In the end, Rahul Kapoor kills Mrignayani's father, means Mehboob Khan's real father. It's a damn good role for Rahul – he gets to kill the main villain. Mehboob Khan kills all the villain's sidekicks, but in the climax, Rahul will get all the claps.'

'Mehboob gets the girl, though,' Mrignayani said, holding a bright yellow dress against herself and posing in front of the mirror. 'How will it look on me?'

'Yummy,' Manoj said, licking his lips exaggeratedly. Mrignayani giggled.

I was still trying to figure out the story. 'But then whose daughter is Mrignayani, really?'

'We still have to decide that,' he said airily. 'That's not very important. We have the basic structure. The details can be worked out later.'

Mrignayani pulled Manoj's hair, making him look at her. 'Oh, so *I* am not important, huh?'

'Ouch, ouch! Jaaneman, the whole film rests on your pretty waist. One jhatka of your kamariya and half of Punjab will forget about sleep for seven days. How does it matter who your father is? In the film, I mean.'

Mrignayani made a face, but ruffled his hair, mollified. What with being pulled and ruffled so much, Manoj's hair was standing on end, looking like a black halo circling his round Gujju face.

'How come the whole script isn't written first?' I asked, wondering whether Munshiji would be writing all the scenes on the sets.

'The main scenes are all fixed. The rest of them will get written as we go along. See, that's Jumbo's power, his grip on the narrative. He's already directed seven films – one super-hit, two hits, one commission-earner and three flops. This one has such a zabardast storyline, it's already been sold in Delhi-Uttar Pradesh territory.'

'But isn't the story a… *bit* clichéd?' I said hesitantly.

'What "bit", it's totally clichéd,' Manoj said earnestly. 'That's the trick of the game. You have to use the clichés in an innovative manner. See, like… You are a woman, you should be able to understand. All women use vegetables and oil and spices to make subzi, right? But the subzi made by two women never tastes exactly the same, right? Same with Hindi films.'

I wondered how Kavita, who was so strait-laced, could have a friend who'd worked in a set-up like this. Then I realised that another friend of hers, namely I, was currently working here. An image of me running down that beautiful, curving road that led out of the set flashed into my head. But then I told myself that I didn't have to ever *see* the film after it was made. As long as it paid the rent...

'I'm learning so much from assisting Jumbo. It's better than any course in film-making,' Manoj said, his eyes on Mrignayani as she posed in front of the mirror.

'Film-making is such a tough job, actually. I don't know how Jambola manages it all,' Mrignayani said seriously. Then she brightened up. 'I'll wear a miniskirt and go and sit in front of Munshiji. It'll give him inspiration.'

I didn't know whether he was deriving inspiration from Mrignayani's copper-coloured leather miniskirt, but Munshiji was writing, slowly, in his notebook. I shifted uncomfortably. I was sitting on the edge of the pavement in the chowk, and the sun was beating straight down on me. We could have sat in the shade of the pine trees, but nobody particularly fancied the idea of being knocked down by another.

Mr Sinha's personal spot boy held a big purple and gold umbrella over his head, but obviously, no such services were available for the assistant directors. Not for the scriptwriter either, though he did have a chair to sit on. I glanced at Munshiji once more. He'd stopped writing.

This wasn't the way things were done in advertising. Not just the script, even the storyboard was prepared in advance, with all the frames drawn and coloured. Even the production was much better organised, at least it was in Mr Bose's company, and I'd never worked anywhere else.

Karan had told me, though, of this set-up where he'd gone to shoot a shampoo ad and they had no water to show the model having a bath. He had smoked five cigarettes, just waiting... He hadn't called back last night. He must've known it was me. I'd waited for half an hour, probably more, sitting by the phone, ready to pick it up at the first ring. What if he'd changed his mind after the phone had rung a few times or if someone else had answered the phone? But he hadn't called up at all. I could feel the tears prickling my eyelids and I was instantly alert. Shit! I couldn't start crying in front of the whole unit, the way I had on Mr Bose's shoot two weeks after the abortion, when Karan wasn't talking to me. Concentrate, I told myself. NOT going to start crying.

It struck me that if I concentrated on not crying, I probably would start crying. Concentrate on the present moment. The past is dead and gone. I remembered what Ma had said once about Papa's death: 'After a while, you realise that the bottom line is that you're just never going to see that person again in your whole life.' And Karan didn't want to see me ever again. Like I were dead or something. The way our baby...

Oh shit, I was making this worse. No. No thinking, not even philosophically. Philosophy was bullshit, anyway. Concentrate on the present, on now.

I looked at the chair in front of me. It was a metal folding chair, painted green. The words on the back – Chandni Production House – were written in small white squiggly letters, spaced far apart in the beginning and then really close, like the painter had realised midway that there wasn't enough space. Good. Very, very good. Keep it up, I told myself. I took in a deep breath and exhaled slowly. Very good. I wasn't about to burst into tears any more. Keep observing. That was the trick.

I looked at another chair. The name of the production house was painted in yellow on this one. A sudden image of Karan painting his name on my forehead flashed into my mind. Grrrr. Back to observing.

I looked up, at the house across the street. It didn't look realistic, but the colour combinations weren't bad. Dark green walls went well with the grey slate roof. Rahul Kapoor was sitting on a chair in front of the house and his silver-coloured shirt set off the dark green, but didn't go too well with his fair complexion. He would probably have looked better in maroon or dark blue. He was wearing dark glasses, a two-day stubble on his chin. His ears were a bit pointed, reminded me of someone... Oh, yes, Mr Spock in *Star Trek*. Sweet lips, though. He didn't have anybody holding an umbrella over his head either, and the sun caught the red highlights in his tousled hair. Karan had taught me how back-light can create a halo around the face... Oh no, not again. Get back to observing. The expanse of Rahul Kapoor's jaw would have looked too broad if it hadn't been broken by the cleft in his chin. His nose was...

Rahul Kapoor took off his glasses and looked straight at me. I blushed and looked away, realising that he'd probably been looking at me while I was observing him.

When I looked back, he gave me a mischievous smile, which made me blush all the more. Good God, I hoped

that he didn't think that I'd been staring at him because
I found him attractive. And all this blushing would just
confirm it.

I turned to look at him and gave him a cool, polite nod.
He nodded back in turn, but the smile was still on his face.
I looked away.

'Cut! OK!' Mr Sinha shouted.

I wrote it down neatly in the continuity book. At long
last, Munshiji had announced that the scene was ready, and
we'd begun shooting. It had gone quite fast after that. Mr
Bose usually took five-six shots in a day, but we'd already
taken seventeen shots in just two hours.

'Rahul was standing to Mrignayani's right in the long
shot. That means his look was Right of Frame. And in the
close shot, he was looking… Left of Frame…' Mr Sinha
said, almost to himself. 'No, how can that be? Hello, what's-
your-name, you've been taking proper care of the continuity,
na?'

'Yes, I have, sir. You're absolutely right, sir. In the long
shot, Rahul Kapoor was standing to Mrignayani's right. In
the close shot, he was looking towards the left of the
frame and in Mrignayani's close shot, she was also looking
towards the left of the frame. I've written it all down
properly, sir,' I said, proudly showing him my continuity
book. I'd decided that a picture was worth a thousand words,
so I'd looked though the movie camera viewfinder before
the shots were taken and sketched the frames. Mr Sinha
stared at my sketches, silently turning the pages. I waited.
The sketches were quite good, actually.

'Manoj!' he bellowed. 'Bhyanchod, what have you done? You want to fuck up my shoot? It's not enough that my stars walk out on me. It's not enough that my producer calls me up at three o'clock in the night. It's not enough that the lab spoils my negatives! My fucking assistants have to be a bunch of incompetent idiots! Fuck up my film, go on, ruin it!'

Manoj hurriedly took the continuity book from Mr Sinha's hands. I stood around, feeling like a fool. It was obvious that I'd made a mistake, but I wasn't sure what it was.

'What happened?' I whispered to Manoj after a while.

'The direction of the actors' looks is not supposed to change from long shot to close shot,' he whispered back.

'Oh,' I said. I hadn't known.

'We'll have to re-shoot shot number 16... 12, 2 and 7. There are some more continuity mistakes as well,' Manoj told me. 'Go, go quickly and do some work on the set. Jumboji is angry.'

I had no idea what I should do. I looked around. Some horses which had been tied to the railing near the chowk had rubbed the yellow paint off it. The paint had been fresh and bright when we started off, so I decided that I wouldn't be disturbing the continuity if I repainted it. I broke into a run, searching for the art direction guys. They seemed to have disappeared, but I managed to find a large collection of paints and brushes of all sizes in the shed where all the props were kept.

I breathed deep, inhaling that typical paint smell. Mmm! That really felt like home. I picked up a can of yellow paint and a brush, and ran back towards the chowk. I'd never claimed to know what writing continuity was all about. So what'd happened wasn't just my fault. But a bad beginning was a bad beginning. I'd have to work doubly hard to prove that I was worth my wages.

Speeding up, I ran around a satin cloth and – Dhapack! I was on the ground with paint dripping on my kurta. And Rahul Kapoor sprawling on my legs.

FOUR

'Omigod,' I said, staring at the yellow paint on his silver-coloured shirt.

'It's OK,' he said reassuringly.

'Of course it's not,' I shrieked, struggling to my feet. 'This is your costume for the scene.'

I tried to wipe the paint off his shirt with my dupatta.

'But your dupatta, it's getting spoilt,' he said.

'Doesn't matter,' I said, dabbing furiously. Fucking up on the continuity was bad enough, but this was simply unforgivable. We were near the shooting area, but I couldn't see Mr Sinha or Manoj because of the satin cloths in the way. I was thankful, since that meant they couldn't see us either.

'Clean it up before it dries,' Mrignayani advised, coming to stand near us.

The dress-men had reached. We made Rahul take off his shirt and then Bihari took charge, rubbing dry-cleaning fluid on it.

'Omigod, there's some paint on your pants as well,' I said, alarmed.

Rahul unzipped his shocking pink pants, and then looked around hesitantly. Everybody was staring at him – Mrignayani, Kapil, even Munshiji from over his half-moon spectacles.

'I'll... uh... do it in the changing room,' Rahul said gruffly.

Mrignayani started giggling as he zipped up his pants and walked off, trying to look dignified. When he turned back to look at us, all of us were laughing.

Manoj stared at me sternly.

'First of all, you shouldn't have bumped into him.'

'Ya, I know, I'm so sorry, but you'd told me to look busy and the thing is, I don't know why, but Rahul Kapoor was running too. In the opposite direction. I ran around the...'

'He was preparing for his shot,' Manoj said curtly, cutting me off in mid-sentence. 'Second, you shouldn't have made him take his clothes off in front of everybody. You're a girl, you should have thought of all this. Third, and most important of all...' Manoj paused for dramatic effect.

'What?' I shifted uneasily. I was aware of Take Two by the Costume Room door, ironing Rahul Kapoor's costume and listening intently to each and every word.

'You shouldn't have laughed at him. Go and apologise to him immediately.'

'Of course I'm sorry that I bumped into him, but what's the big deal about *laughing*? Everybody was laughing. He actually unzipped...'

'Don't you know about stars and their egos?' Manoj snapped. 'You have to put them on a pedestal, pamper them.

They're all dumbos, but they're moody dumbos. If a star throws a tantrum, it's our shooting that gets fucked. Look at how Mehboob Khan walked out of our shoot today.'

I nodded, remembering the way Manoj had kept on pleading with Mehboob Khan while the star was throwing all those ma-bahen ki gaalis at him.

'But you're so casual with Mrignayani,' I realised suddenly.

'This is her first film, that's why we can treat her any way we feel like,' Manoj said coldly. 'She needs us, we don't need her.'

I knocked at the door of Rahul Kapoor's changing room, holding his freshly-ironed costume in my hands. I'd thought that I was too good to work in a set-up like this, and I'd already made two fuck-ups in a single day. If I carried on this way, I was soon going to find myself with the sack.

Rahul Kapoor opened the door and looked at me enquiringly. He was wearing dark blue jeans and a towel strung around his neck. I could see a faint yellow mark on his bare chest. I wasn't sure whether offering him dry cleaning fluid to clean it up would be a good idea, so I didn't.

'Your costume. The dress-men have removed all the stains,' I said nervously, wondering whether he was going to start abusing me like Mehboob Khan had abused Manoj. 'I'm so, so sorry.'

'About what?' he said, taking the costume from me and folding his arms.

'About... uh... bumping into you,' I said, fingering my kurta where the yellow paint had left a light stain, in spite of Take Two's ministrations.

He stared at me.

'And, like, about making you take off your pants. And about laughing at you. I'm sorry.' I'd said it.

'I'll forgive you,' he said seriously. 'On one condition.'

'What?' I said.

'Have coffee with me tonight.' His face broke into a grin.

I was flabbergasted, but I managed to come up with an 'I'd rather stay unforgiven,' and walked off.

I had one more apology to tender that day.

'I'm so sorry, sir, about the continuity mistakes,' I said timidly to Mr Sinha after we'd packed up for the day.

'What "sir-sir"? Call me Jumbo,' Mr Sinha said, giving me a friendly slap on the back.

'Uh...yes, so, I'm very sorry...'

'Jumbo, Jumbo,' he said, smiling into my eyes. 'Your friendly neighbourhood elephant. You can even call me Jambola, like our Mrignayani.'

Jambola, my foot. But I decided that I might as well call him Jumbo, since everyone else did. This wasn't the corporate sector, this was the Hindi film industry. Why be different and stick out?

'I'm sorry about the continuity mistakes, Jumbo,' I said, then remembered what Manoj called him. 'Sorry, I mean *Jumboji*.' How could I have forgotten the mandatory ji?

'The continuity mistake was my fault,' Manoj said, coming forward gallantly. 'I assigned the continuity to her without confirming that she knows what to do.'

'But I thought that you'd worked as an assistant director in that what's-the-name... Pink Light Films,' Jumbo (nee Mr Sinha) said vaguely, fanning himself with the red check gamchha that was always strung around his neck.

'Bose Productions. I worked there for six months, but not as an assistant director. I was an assistant production designer. I didn't have anything to do with writing continuity.'

'OK, OK,' Jumbo said, losing interest. 'Have a paan, very nice paans I have, very refreshing. Here, a special Nagina paan for you.'

He picked out a silver-covered paan from his paan-box and held it out to me like it was a delicacy.

'I don't eat paan, sir...' I said uncertainly.

Jumbo looked a bit hurt, but said, 'No problem, whatever you like. Be comfortable, feel free, if there's any problem, tell Manoj, or come to me. Feel free.'

He offered the paan to Mrignayani who bent down and ate it out of his hand, treating us to a brief flash of cleavage. The gamchha slipped from Jumbo's hand and I started to bend down instinctively, but I stopped myself. 'If you're too nice to people, they'll treat you like shit,' Sharmishtha used to chide me when I first joined Mr Bose's office. Manoj and Mrignayani banged their heads against each other as they bent down to pick up the gamchha. Manoj got to it first and handed it to Jumbo, who hadn't even bothered to bend down.

'Special paan for you, today,' Jumbo rewarded Manoj and gave him a big, bright green one.

Manoj smiled gratefully. Then he bit into it – and the smile disappeared. I could see the tears appear in Manoj's eyes, but he continued chewing manfully.

'What's in it?' I asked Manoj after Jumbo had left with Mrignayani in his bright red Mercedes.

'Tobacco,' he gasped. 'An especially... strong one.'

'Thank God I didn't eat it,' I said.

'Oh, he wouldn't have given you one with tobacco, you're a girl,' he said. 'You should have taken it. It was a big honour, Jumbo offering you a paan on your first day of work.'

'My first day of work.' I shook my head ruefully. 'I'm still feeling so bad about the continuity mistakes. It was nice of you to take the blame, but Jumbo must be thinking...'

'Hey, don't think so much. Jumbo's a cool guy. And anyway, you're a girl, so he won't hold these small mistakes against you.' Manoj spat out the paan into a potted plant, and relaxed a bit.

The guard at the entrance of the set was arguing with two teenage girls, but he snapped to attention and saluted Manoj when we passed him. The girls approached us shyly.

'Mehboob Khan is there?' one of them said, showing us an autograph book.

'Mehboob has left. But, yes, that other hero is there – Rahul Kapoor. Go, take his autograph,' Manoj said.

The girls tossed a gleeful look at the guard and walked into the car park, heads held high. Manoj laughed and waved at Rahul Kapoor who was trying to start a small, run-down jeep. Rahul Kapoor waved back and gave me a brilliant smile – to which I responded with a cool nod.

'Jumbo blew up today because he was stressed out by Mehboob Khan's walking out. These bloody stars! Jumbo took it today, but he'll get back at him, just you watch. Jumbo's quite a biggie himself now. Last year, when the income tax department conducted raids on all the top people in the industry, his house was also raided,' Manoj told me as we walked down the curving road to the bus stop at the bottom of the hill.

'Ya?' I said. 'How much money did they find?'

'Fourteen lakhs,' Manoj said proudly. 'They found forty-seven lakhs at Mehboob Khan's place, but still, fourteen lakhs is not a small amount.'

'Yes.'

We sat down on a railing near the bus stop. The picture-perfect rolling green hills that stretched out as far as I could see looked vaguely familiar. I'd probably seen them in some films.

'I hope you don't mind,' Manoj said chivalrously, taking out a pack of cigarettes.

'Not at all,' I said, and took a cigarette. He looked surprised, but didn't say anything. I used to smoke once in a while with Karan, just because I enjoyed the companionship of smoking with him. Even now, I didn't particularly feel like smoking. I was just fed up with Manoj's 'you're a girl' attitude.

He lit my cigarette. I was careful not to take the smoke into my lungs – coughing in front of him would be too much of a loss of face.

'I think women who smoke look really cool,' Manoj said warmly. 'If you analyse it in a Freudian way, a phallic symbol between a woman's lips looks much more appropriate than a man's. What do you think?'

What? Manoj looked much too serious and sincere for me to take offence, but I hurriedly changed the subject. 'This Rahul Kapoor, if he's a star, how come he drives such a khatara jeep?'

'Obviously he's not such a big star as Mehboob Khan. He's just two releases old, so he hasn't earned much money yet. How do I explain his status to you? See, like, Rahul doesn't rate an air-conditioned make-up van, but he does rate a changing room of his own. With an AC. All of us can call him Rahul, that's cool, but we have to call Mehboob Khan "Mehboobji" to his face.'

'And to his back?'

'"Bhyanchod."' Manoj grinned. 'Don't take tension, you'll soon figure out the power equations here. Tell me, have you seen Rahul Kapoor's *Maut Ke Sikandar*?'

'Uh, no.' I hadn't even heard of it.

'His first film. Big hit. But it had four heroes in it. And his solo film was a flop. So he's not hot right now, but with this industry it doesn't take much time for what's down to come up and what's up to go down.'

'What about Mrignayani?' I said suddenly. 'What if she becomes a star?'

'Right now she's giving me bhav because my Dad's a distributor, but once she's established – she won't even bother to recognise me. Or maybe she'll deign to wave at me from her Lamborghini when she's passing by.' Manoj shrugged.

'Lamborghini, hmm?' I smiled. 'I've never even seen a Lamborghini. What's your dream car?'

'You ask so many questions. Like a journalist. But I don't mind, why should I mind talking to a pretty girl like you?' he said with a wink. 'I've got an Opel Astra at home. But I want to travel in locals, in buses. If I don't go through the same trials and tribulations that the common man does, how can I make a film for him?'

He sounded really very serious about this whole endeavour.

The bus seemed to be a good training ground for Manoj. It was so packed, there was barely enough place to stand.

'Don't worry, Madam, you'll get a seat in Gokuldham,' Take Two, who was standing behind me, said.

'Is the bus always so crowded?' I asked, wondering whether I'd have to stand in the bus everyday.

'Today we packed up at six, that's why it's so crowded,' Take Two explained. 'Usually we'll pack up at ten. The bus is quite empty then. But the only problem is, we have to wait for it for an hour.'

'Oh,' I said. As it is, my place was just ten kilometres away, but this bus would only take us to Goregaon railway station. From there I'd have to take a local train to Andheri, and then another bus home.

'But don't ever walk to the Film City gate alone at night if the bus is late,' Manoj cautioned. 'Leopards roam around in this area sometimes.'

'Leopards?'

'I saw this big leopard just last week,' Take Two chimed in. 'During a night shoot. It was sitting on a branch and snarling at me. I didn't get scared, I just...'

'Don't believe a word he says,' Bihari said gruffly. 'He's a pukka liar.'

'Ya, ya, don't worry.' Manoj hastened to reassure me. 'Nothing is going to happen, but there's no harm in being careful, is there?'

I peered out of a window. There were no streetlights on the road that wound through rich green grassland, and I could imagine leopards lurking in the tall grass. Good God, leopards of all the things in the world! I knew I'd landed up at the wrong place.

That night, after I made a blank call to Karan, I didn't wait for him to call back. All I wanted to do was hear his voice. I was so tired, I didn't even have the energy to argue with myself about why I needed to call him. The landlady's twelve-year-old son had eaten up the chivda that my mother had sent with me, and there was nothing to eat in our room except a month-old packet of chikki. I sat on a chair and steadily ate it up. It probably wasn't doing me much good, but it was sweet, and things being as they were, I needed all the comfort I could get.

I would have fallen asleep immediately, but Shweta was playing Metallica at full volume. I tossed and turned, trying to sleep, but it was impossible. I burrowed my head into the pillow and covered my ears with it. That seemed to help somewhat, but then I started to suffocate.

I let myself fantasise about systematically dismantling Shweta's music system and breaking each part with a hammer. But when I finally fell asleep, I didn't dream of Shweta's music system or even of Karan. I dreamt of Mrignayani dancing under a waterfall with a big black buffalo, while Mehboob Khan played the drums.

FIVE

I was so fed up with Rahul Kapoor, I was quite glad when the monkey bit him. As soon as the monkey was brought on the set, Rahul had announced that he loved animals very much and started making friendly overtures, but the monkey refused to give him any bhav. He (the monkey, that is) had been quite restless all morning. His owner hadn't fed him anything because he was supposed to eat from Rahul's hands during the shot.

Rahul's make-up man touched up his make-up and brushed his hair into studied disarray like he did before every take. The monkey owner deposited the monkey on Rahul's lap and disappeared as Jumbo called out, 'Roll camera!'

'Rolling,' shouted the assistant cameraman.

'Action!' Jumbo ordered.

The monkey growled when Rahul tried to pet him, and before any of us realised what was happening, Rahul was jumping around, yelping, with the monkey hanging from his arm.

'Cut, cut, cut!' Jumbo yelled.

The monkey left Rahul's arm and ran to his owner, who was running towards him. The owner picked him up and talked to him soothingly as he clung to the man's shirt, chattering complainingly like a child.

'You shouldn't have jerked your hand away when he took it in his mouth,' the owner told Rahul. 'He felt startled and that's why he bit you.'

'Oh, is that why?' Rahul said sceptically.

'Monkey cancel,' Jumbo announced. 'Munshiji, write in a cat instead.'

'I'm so sorry,' Manoj apologised to Rahul. 'We should have been more careful. Who the fuck got this monkey?'

Kapil took one step back. 'The production manager took me to this place...'

'I guess I'll have to take rabies shots now,' Rahul grumbled as I dressed his wound. 'I had to take fourteen shots in my stomach once, when I was a kid – a puppy I'd got home from the streets bit me.'

'No, no, don't worry,' I reassured him. 'I checked with the owner. The monkey's already taken rabies shots.'

He looked at me crossly.

'Why should the monkey take rabies shots? I didn't bite him.'

I stared at him for a moment, not understanding, and then, burst out laughing.

'The monkey,' I said, between peals of laughter, 'took the shot before it bit you. A vaccine. So you don't have to worry about rabies or anything.'

'Oh, like that,' he said gruffly.

Manoj gestured to me with his eyes to stop laughing.

'But you should go to a doctor and get a tetanus shot,' I said, biting back my laughter. 'Get it bandaged properly as well.'

'You've bandaged it with so much love, what more do I need?' he said, smiling at me in what was supposed to be an engaging manner.

Grrr. I didn't say anything but I pressed a swab of Dettol on the bite. Manoj had forbidden me from being rude to Rahul Kapoor. According to Manoj, assistant directors were not required to have egos. 'Thoda adjust karna padta hai, Paro,' he'd tell me regularly.

'Aiyaiyo, amma! You can't imagine how much it hurts. But if you hold my hand and look into my eyes, the pain will fly away,' Rahul said, blowing air on my ear as I bent down to tie the bandage.

'How about coffee tonight?' he added hopefully.

'I don't drink coffee,' I said shortly.

'How about tea? How about me?'

Good God! Did he think he was being witty or something? His main problem was that he was convinced that he was God's gift to womankind. He was so used to women falling for him, he expected that with one soulful look and a flash of dimples, he could sweep any girl off her feet.

Right from my first day of work, when I'd bumped into him, he'd launched this full-scale effort to patao me. He'd declared that since the hero and heroine bumping into each other was the time-honoured way for Hindi film romances to begin, we were meant to be together. He seemed to think that his flirting was charming, but I found it extremely irritating. I snubbed him discreetly because Manoj had warned me enough times about offending the stars. Anyway, my snubs didn't seem to make much difference to Rahul – his grin was irrepressible.

As I straightened up, Rahul pulled out the jooda pin from my hair. My hands flew to stop it but my hair came loose. Rahul shook the pin so that the little bells at the end of it tinkled. Karan had brought this pin for me back from a shoot in Rajasthan. Seeing it in this brash actor's hand seemed like sacrilege. I reached out for it and he pulled his hand back a little. I stretched and just as my hand touched the pin, he held it up above his head.

I put my hands on my hips and glared at him. He looked chastened and offered me the pin, swinging it so that the bells tinkled. I reached out quickly to grab it, but with a laugh he threw it up and caught it.

I stalked off. I felt a hand on my shoulder and turned around, ready to blast Rahul, but my face broke into a huge grin when I saw that it was Saira behind me.

'You're looking very pretty in pink,' I said, looking her up and down. 'Pink saree, pink bindi, my God, even your sandals are pink!'

'And you're looking very dowdy in brown. Your salwar kurta is so loose, it could fit me,' Saira said disapprovingly.

'I don't want anybody to look at me. Why the fuck should I bother about looking attractive?' I said, making a face, and linked arms with her to lead her to the table where tea was served.

'Somebody does find you attractive all the same,' Saira said with a smile, gesturing with her eyes to Rahul Kapoor who was leaning on a pillar in the temple, playing with the tinkling bells on my jooda pin. 'My God, he's so handsome, how can you ignore him like this?'

'He's an actor, he's supposed to be good-looking,' I said coolly. Then, to be fair, I added, 'But he's not as dumb as I thought. He said something really thought-provoking yesterday – "The necessity to eat does not justify the prostitution of Art." Munshiji, our scriptwriter, liked it a lot. He immediately translated it into Hindi. Says it'll make a dhamakedaar dialogue.'

'Bunuel said that.'

'Said what?' I asked, confused.

'That "necessity to eat" one. It's a quote. By Luis Bunuel. He's a European film-maker. He made these really funny surrealistic films. There's this film he made with Salvador Dali in which an eye is cut open in front of the camera. It really gives you a jhatka when you see it for the first time…'

Rahul Kapoor slid off his dark glasses with my jooda pin and gave me a look that was probably meant to give me a jhatka. Trust an actor to pass off other people's words as his own, I thought. I wanted to show him my tongue, but Manoj's admonitions stopped me. I put on the most bored expression I could muster and looked away disdainfully.

I took Saira around the set, showing her the meandering streets and the façade of the church and the slate-roofed cottages, especially Mehboob Khan's cottage, in front of which I'd got a verandah constructed. The art director's team had worked really hard on the verandah, draping bougainvillaea all around it to give it a hint of privacy. Jumbo had declared the place very romantic and shot three scenes here.

'Hmm,' Saira said. 'It *is* very romantic. You should drag Rahul Kapoor here one lazy afternoon and have a long smooching session with him.'

'Don't be silly,' I snapped.

'OK,' Saira shrugged and lit a cigarette.

'What's your new boyfriend like?' I asked, trying to make up. Saira had taken a new job two weeks ago and found a new boyfriend one week ago. To celebrate both, she was taking Kavita and me out tonight to 'Not Just Jazz by the Bay', a nightclub in South Bombay.

'He's such fun! He's absolutely crazy,' Saira said, perking up immediately. 'He makes me laugh so much, my tummy hurts.'

'What does he do for a living?' I asked, leaning on a railing.

'He directs promos for a music channel. He's very creative,' she said. 'His real name is Dilip, but everybody calls him Whacko.'

'Whacko!' I laughed. 'Watch out!'

'He's crazy in a very sweet way. Guess what he gave me as a together-for-a-week present?'

'What?'

'Seven heart-shaped magnets,' she laughed delightedly and then suddenly became serious. 'What about you? How are you feeling now – about Karan?'

'I'll survive,' I said flippantly. 'Nobody dies of heartbreak.'

'Ya, I should know, I've been through so many of them,' Saira said, shaking her head. 'But how are you... otherwise?'

I knew that she was referring to the abortion, but somehow, although I knew that she was asking because she cared, I just didn't want to talk about it.

'I'm fine now, well on my way to getting over everything.' I smiled brightly, but I didn't know whether she believed me. I wasn't doing so bad, actually. I still found the film ridiculous, and Rahul Kapoor was a pain in the ass, but otherwise, work was okey-dokey. The best thing about assisting was that it left me with little time to brood over Karan and the abortion. I'd even managed to cut down the blank calls to twice a week. I could smile, I even laughed, just that there was a hole in my gut that refused to go away.

The last place that I showed Saira was my Costume Room. It was a funny thing, the way it had become 'my' Costume Room in the one month that I'd been working there.

When we walked in, Manoj was lying on a couple of tin trunks, trying to ignore Mrignayani who was rifling though the costumes hung above him.

'Mannoo!' Mrignayani complained. 'I'm going to look like a beggar-girl in the film.'

'Let me sleep,' Manoj mumbled.

'I don't have any clothes to wear.'

'Don't wear any clothes, then,' Manoj said, smiling with his eyes closed. Mrignayani dropped a green satin dress on his face, but he refused to react, just kept on sleeping.

Saira was looking around the costume room, a little dazed.

'It's... colourful,' she said finally.

'Yes, it is,' I grinned. 'But take a look at this.'

I opened a tin trunk and showed her our huge collection of white shoes and sandals and slippers and mojris.

'The hero in Jumbo's first film wore white shoes and that film was a silver jubilee hit, so he makes all the stars in his film wear white shoes – they're his lucky mascot,' I told her. 'Mehboob Khan has more than twenty white shoes in different styles to go with his costumes. Look.'

Saira oohed and aahed over the white shoes and the assorted accessories that I showed her, but what she found most interesting was Mrignayani's bosom.

'Are they real?' Saira whispered to me.

I shook my head and she grinned, happy. Mrignayani saw her grinning and smiled back. When Mrignayani found out that Saira was a journalist, she was even more friendly.

'Oh, it must be so difficult, being a journalist. I'm sure I could never go around interviewing people all day and writing it all down later. Writing is so tough – look at poor Munshiji,' Mrignayani said breathlessly.

'I'm sure it's not very easy being an actress either,' Saira said in turn.

Mrignayani nodded. 'Everybody thinks it's easy money – you just go in front of the camera and wriggle your hips. But there's so much competition, you can't imagine. There are at least a thousand struggling actors for every role.'

Mrignayani sat down on a tin trunk near Saira, glad to have found a sympathetic ear.

'You have such a nice name – Mrignayani,' Saira said.

'You like it? I like it. There was a character in a serial named Mrignayani. I got it from there. A mythological serial,' Mrignayani told her. 'These guys wanted me to change it to something shorter, but I put my foot down.'

'It's different, probably makes you stand out from the competition,' Saira said. And then, with typical Sagittarian aplomb, she asked, 'I've heard all these stories about the casting couch. Do you really have to sleep with producers to get roles?'

I wanted the earth to open up and swallow me. I tried to cover up, but Mrignayani didn't seem to have taken any offence.

'Of course it happens. Even men have to do it, you know. There are so many gay producers around nowadays,' Mrignayani said.

'Well, that should be cool for you, then. You can just go and meet all the gay producers,' Saira suggested practically.

'I wish. That's not the way it works, though. There are so many other people around, right from directors, to stars, to cameramen... I've heard, for *Jaan Ka Dushman* – there's this new girl, Rashmi, in it – well, she had to sleep with everybody. Anybody in the unit who wanted to could fuck her – right from the producer to the spot boys.'

'Spot boys?' I asked, incredulous.

'The unit which fucks together, sticks together,' Manoj said, from under the green satin dress.

Mrignayani threw a white shoe at him. 'You're supposed to be sleeping.'

'Sometimes I think that I'm being too condescending but… what to do, that set-up really is incredible,' I said to Kavita after Saira had narrated the guys-have-to-do-it-too story over a stiff vodka martini at 'Not Just Jazz by the Bay'.

'I'm feeling very guilty about sending you to a place like that,' Kavita said.

'I've always wondered how *you* know somebody who's worked there as an assistant director,' I said. Kavita was a computer programmer, and the only 'artistic types' she knew were Saira and me.

'Oh, Abhijeet knows Michael from his college,' Kavita said. 'He never told me about all this sleazy business, though. If I'd known, I would never have suggested this job to you.'

'It's OK. It pays the rent,' I said and laughed. 'It doesn't pay much else, but it pays the rent.'

'Don't look at the prices tonight,' Saira said expansively. 'Just order whatever you feel like.'

'Don't think of calories tonight,' I smiled. 'Just order whatever you feel like.'

'No, baba. I'm not getting off my diet now. I'm just five kgs away from my goal;' Saira said. 'Do you know, that fellow Manoj, he said that I'm very pretty. He even asked me out for dinner.'

'When? I mean, when did he do that?' I asked, surprised.

'Oh, when you'd gone to arrange for the blocks of ice for tomorrow's shoot. I said no, of course.'

'That makes seven,' I said. I took a cigarette from Saira's pack and explained. 'You're the seventh girl who's turned him down this month. He's developed a very practical attitude towards rejections. He sat down and calculated one day that, on an average, out of every eleven girls he asks out, one says yes. So he tries to collect as many rejections as he can – it means that an acceptance is bound to pop up soon.'

'Many are the uses of statistics,' said Kavita, who'd done her graduation in statistics. 'Are you included in this seven?'

'He's generally a little lechy, and he did make a sort-of pass at me as well, but didn't take it personally when I refused,' I said. 'He thinks it would be very rude of him not to make a pass at every girl he meets. He doesn't want anybody to feel unwanted.'

'Oh, so he's making passes at all the girls out of the kindness of his heart, huh? Noble soul,' Kavita commented.

'What about Mrignayani? Is anything happening between them?' Saira asked.

'I doubt it. Mrignayani is too busy fucking Jumbo to have an affair with Manoj. She enjoys flirting with him, though. Manoj says that he flirts with her just out of politeness. She'd be very insulted if every man she met didn't fall in lust with her.'

'Really? He's not the least bit interested in her, huh?' Saira said.

'I'm sure he wouldn't mind fucking her if she let him,' I said. 'He'll have his fun in the industry and then go home and marry a nice Gujju girl his mother chooses for him. "Nice girl" means an unfucked virgin, I suppose.'

'You're using a lot of swear words nowadays, Parvati,' Kavita said, her gentle voice an admonishment.

'Ya, that's what it's all about – fucking. I've given up on euphemisms,' I said.

'Men don't like women who swear,' Kavita said.

'Sure. The same kind of men who want to fuck around and then go and marry virgins,' I said, irritated.

'All Indian men want to marry virgins,' Kavita asserted.

'Well, I'm not a virgin now, so I guess nobody's going to want to marry me,' I said, trying to sound flippant.

'What hogwash! Times have changed, darlings!' Saira was charged high, with her new job and even newer boyfriend.

'What "changed"?' Kavita said. 'The census report shows that there are only 861 females to every thousand males in Haryana.'

'What's Haryana got to do with me?' Saira said. 'I'm talking about here, now. Bombay.'

'You think well-educated guys don't have double standards? You know my brother, Pradeep? He's in America. I was talking to him on the phone two days back and *he* said that he wants to marry a virgin,' Kavita said, taking a sip of her Bloody Mary.

'Well, I'm not going around with your brother.' Saira bit into her roasted papad.

'Do you think that the guys you go around with will tell you this?' Kavita said.

'The guys I go around with are... different.' Saira's voice was definitely clipped now.

'How many of these guys have asked you to marry them? Hmm?'

Saira opened her mouth, but before she could start shouting, I interjected, 'Girls, girls, no fighting now.'

We sipped our drinks in silence for a while. Why did Kavita and Saira have to argue every time we met? I sighed and looked around. Most of the tables in the dimly-lit nightclub were occupied by couples. We were the only women who were sitting by ourselves. The only women without men. But, aha, the couple at the next table was fighting. At least I wasn't in a shitty relationship.

'What, yaar!' Kavita complained. 'Saira's attitudes keep on changing according to what's happening in her love life. Two months ago, after Sameer left her, she went around saying that all men are bastards. Now, she's found some guy, she's gone gaga over the male race. She should have a consistent worldview, na?'

'Manview,' I said, smiling.

'Why do we talk so much about men, anyway?' Kavita said tiredly.

'Ya, I know,' Saira said, perking up. 'Let's talk about, say, politics. Or food. A friend of mine tried the General Motors diet and she swears that it really works. She lost...'

'Why should we talk about dieting?' I interrupted. 'That's related to men as well.'

'I completely agree,' Kavita said. 'We should just kick men out of our lives.'

Neither Saira nor I said anything. Actually, Kavita needed to kick just one guy out of her life. For the past four years, she'd been involved with a married man. She gave him ultimatums – your wife or me – but he couldn't make up his mind, and when it came to the crunch, Kavita couldn't leave him. It wasn't as if she hadn't tried hard enough – every once in a while she'd tell him it was over, date other men to get over him, refuse to even talk to him. Last year, when his wife had had a baby, Kavita had even changed her job and her paying guest place without telling him. But nothing worked. Like a spring, the further they'd been from each other, the closer they'd get when they came together again.

'How's Abhijeet?' I asked Kavita.

She didn't reply immediately, just held up her half-empty glass and looked at us through it.

'I've been going to a psychotherapist,' she said abruptly. 'To help me break up with Abhijeet.'

Saira was as startled by this as I was.

'For how long... have you been going to this psychiatrist?' I asked hesitantly.

'Psychotherapist, not psychiatrist. Two weeks – four sessions. It's not so bad.'

'No, no, not bad... I guess.' I didn't know anybody else who'd ever been to a psychotherapist.

'I also felt very awkward at first,' Kavita said. 'You know how it is. Abroad, it's a fashion to go to shrinks. Here... Forget about other people, when I was sitting in the waiting room, I kept on sneaking glances at the other patient and thinking, "Hey, better be careful, this man might be a nutcase. What if he gets up and smashes this coffee-table on my head?"'

'It must have taken a lot of guts,' Saira said. 'But did it... help any?'

'Majorly. I got this insight… how do I explain to you? Like, I'd always been blaming Abhijeet for whatever was happening, right? I realised that I'm just as responsible. OK, Abhijeet is a bastard, my ex-boyfriend was also a bastard, but why did *I* have to get involved with men like that? The shrink made me realise that my pattern of falling for married men goes down to the time when Papa left Mama for that woman. I subconsciously keep on choosing a man like my father who is being unfaithful to his wife.'

'But I don't understand one thing,' Saira said slowly. 'If you had to choose someone like your father, you could have *married* a guy like that. Why did you have to be the other woman?'

'You're absolutely right. I also asked my shrink that. He says that I've got this deep-rooted fear of commitment. I was just nine years old when Papa left us and nobody thought that I understood anything. I didn't know too much, because they didn't tell me anything. But based on whatever information I had, plus the fact that it hurt so much, I subconsciously decided that I didn't want to ever put myself into the position where somebody walking out on me could shatter my world, just like that. If everything seems to be certain and permanent in a relationship, I couldn't take it if things broke up. That's why I had to subconsciously choose a guy who couldn't give me a commitment. A married man really fits the bill, na?'

'But… but, if you apply the same logic to me, it means that I chose Karan knowing that he's going to ditch me,' I argued.

'You probably did,' Kavita countered.

'Hey, what nonsense,' Saira said, sitting back. 'Why would she *choose* to fuck up her own happiness this way?'

'I'm not a psychotherapist, I don't *know*, but I think that a deep-rooted fear of commitment is the problem for all of us. Because of what we went through as children,' Kavita said.

I took a sip of my Virgin Mary, thinking about what she'd said. One of the things that had drawn the three of us together was that we all came from, well, if not broken homes, then not normal, one-mama, one-papa kind of happy homes either. My mother had brought up my two sisters and me all by herself after our father died when I was seven years old. Kavita's father had left her mother to marry another woman. Saira's parents were not divorced or anything, but they fought so bitterly, she wished they were.

'Uh, what about me?' Saira said, a little worried.

'Well, the way I analyse it is that you feel so scared of having a bad marriage, you've formed a pattern of having short-lived, intense relationships,' Kavita said. 'You say that you want to get married but – I hope you don't mind my saying this...'

'No, no, not at all, it's OK,' Saira said, leaning forward. 'But what...'

'But you've been sabotaging your relationships subconsciously,' Kavita said. 'You set yourself up. You find a guy who you know, subconsciously, is not compatible with you. Or once you're involved, you subconsciously behave in such a way that...'

'What's this "subconscious-subconscious" business, yaar,' I said. 'I'm not sold on the idea. And anyway, how can you reach the conclusion that all of us have this pattern? I've had just one relationship.'

'You've just started, Paro,' Kavita said. 'And that graphic design teacher you had a crush on – he was also unavailable, wasn't he?'

'Oh, like that.' I munched on the idea for a while.

'But how do I find out whether I'm actually... you know, subconsciously, thinking like that?' Saira said, confused.

'That's what you need a shrink for,' Kavita said.

'Well, how much does going to a shrink cost?' Saira asked.

'Mine charges three hundred rupees per session,' Kavita told her.

'Maybe I should go and treat myself to a session sometime,' Saira said thoughtfully. 'You know, like a facial.'

'You definitely should. We all should,' Kavita said earnestly. 'It's much more important than facials and you're right, it costs that much only. Just think, why do we have facials, so that we can attract men, right? But what's the point if we keep on attracting the wrong kind of guys into our lives? It'll help us to be OK, not just look OK. From inside.'

'So we'll attract the right kind of guys. Hmm, ya,' Saira sipped her drink, thinking seriously, then looked up at Kavita. 'What does your shrink look like?'

'Saira!' Kavita hung her head in exasperation.

'What did I say, what did I say?' Saira said indignantly as both Kavita and I started laughing. 'I just wanted to *visualise* him, that's...'

I patted her arm. 'Don't worry, maybe you'll get what you're looking for. A friend of a friend of mine went to this New Age shrink who believes in very unconventional therapy. She walked into his office and told him that she'd come to him because she'd got a problem. He told her to take off all her clothes.'

'And she did?' Saira said, her eyes round with surprise.

'Obviously. Therapy, no,' Kavita chimed in.

'Then what happened,' Saira said.

'Then he told her to lie down on the couch,' I continued. 'Very proper Freudian couch and all he's got. So she lay down on it, like a good little girl. He took off his clothes, put them on top of hers and got on the couch and – I'd say screwed, but Kavita would disapprove. So, he had sexual intercourse with her. Then he got up, put on his clothes and said to her, "Now that we've solved my problem, let's solve yours."'

Saira smiled sheepishly while Kavita and I laughed our guts out.

'Hey, I know this really good one,' Saira said, trying to cover up her sheepishness. 'There's this shrink...'

'And he's tall and dark and handsome and he's got a voice like Amitabh Bachchan's,' I said, leaning towards her.

'I won't bore you with the joke if you don't want to hear it,' Saira said, miffed.

'I was just pulling your leg, baba,' I cajoled her. 'Of course we...'

I stopped suddenly, completely. Karan was standing in front of me, just a few feet away. He hadn't noticed me, in fact he was turning away from me to pull out a chair, when a waiter directed him to another table. I wanted to call out to him, but my tongue felt paralysed. Karan turned to touch the waist of a girl who was standing near him, leading her to the other table. They had to pass by our side and I wanted to look away, but I couldn't and then, he'd seen me.

'Hi!' he said, and stopped suddenly.

'Hi,' I managed to say.

He greeted Kavita and Saira politely and introduced us to the girl who was standing by his side – Deepti Chawla. I remembered her vaguely – she used to work for Blue Moon, an advertising agency. I forced myself to give her a smile and looked away.

'Where are you working nowadays?' Karan asked me politely.

'I'm working as an assistant director on a Hindi film,' I said, and took a sip of my Virgin Mary. That was a mistake. My throat had closed up on me, I could barely swallow.

'Oh, wow, that must be interesting,' he said.

'Very, yes, interesting.'

'Be seeing you then. Bye!'

'Bye!' I replied.

He nodded at Kavita and Saira, and moved on.

'You were very… dignified,' Kavita said.

I nodded. For the past two months, I'd been yearning desperately to meet him, to be with him, to talk to him. And now, finally, I'd met him and we'd talked, in a very dignified and very polite way. Very, very polite, like one would with an acquaintance. I held myself tight, trying to breathe deep, but two humiliating tears crept out of my left eye and crawled down my cheek. I brushed them away, trying to look casual.

'Let's leave,' Kavita said.

'Why should we leave,' I said, biting the insides of my cheeks and looking away. 'What were we talking about, oh yes...'

'Ya, so, there's this shrink...' Saira began quickly. I could tell that Karan had sat down a few tables behind us because Kavita's eyes followed him, then looked back at me.

I sat up straight. I wouldn't turn around, I wouldn't. The back of my neck ached with tension. I knew him so well, I didn't even have to look to know what he was doing. He must be leaning forward, holding, not her hand, but her bracelet, playing with it, whispering so that she had to lean forward as well. I could feel his touch on my wrist, caressing... I jerked my hand up, and because I had to do something with it, ran it through my hair.

'...and she sat in front of him, eating cucumbers,' Saira said.

I broke into laughter. I wasn't sure whether that had been the punchline, but Kavita and Saira joined me, laughing along loudly.

I suddenly realised that Karan might be looking at me, so I started to tell a joke animatedly. I could see from Kavita's and Saira's faces that what I was saying wasn't making much sense, but they went along, smiling and nodding.

This was so damn dumb, anybody could see through it, especially Karan, he knew me so well. But maybe he wasn't looking at me at all, he was just concentrating on Deepti Chawla. She'd got a big waist, I remembered. But big boobs as well. Maybe that compensated. Karan had always said that I'd got the best boobs in the whole world. Maybe he said that to every girl. I imagined him caressing Deepti's boobs and I felt vomit rush into my throat.

'I've got to go,' I said, getting up abruptly. 'No, no, don't come with me, you just... enjoy your evening. Bye!'

The local train was so crowded, I barely got a place to stand in the door. I clutched the rod in the middle of the door, staring out at the bright silver railway track. Sometimes I felt like letting go of the rod, just letting go, that's all I'd have to do. Gravity would do the rest. I'd definitely die, wouldn't I? I remembered reading somewhere that an average of 8.39 people died on the railway tracks in Bombay every day. Just another statistic read over breakfast.

But it wouldn't be just another statistic for Ma, back home in Amravati, would it? I clutched the rod more tightly and turned to push my way in, into the thick mass of women.

SIX

'Cut! N.G.!' Jumbo called out.

'N.G.,' I noted down in the continuity book. No Good. I was probably N.G. for Karan now. And Deepti was OK. Why didn't Karan love me any more? It didn't make much sense, but – why couldn't God have made Karan love me? What difference would it have made to Him? Just a little adjustment to the divine transmogrifier (or whatever) and Karan would never have left me.

But wait a minute, how long had their affair been going on? Hadn't Mr Bose said that Karan was fucking around behind my back? But he'd probably said it so that he could get me.

In fact, it wasn't even necessary that just because Karan and Deepti had come together to the restaurant, there was something going on between them. But he'd touched her waist when the waiter had directed them to another table. And he'd played with her bracelet when they were sitting together. No, that I had just imagined, hadn't...

'Cut! N.G.!' Jumbo shouted.

Oh, shit! I'd missed watching this take. I quickly scribbled in the continuity book. Thank God, it was an N.G. take, the continuity didn't really matter. But it had to be noted down, so that the laboratory didn't print it.

'You have to fall properly, baby,' Jumbo admonished Mrignayani, falling on the road with a big thump. 'Like this, see, don't bend your knees.'

I reminded myself that I had to go and check whether the art director's team had made the pushcarts of lightweight wood which would be broken during the fight scene. I looked at my watch. 10:20. Maybe Karan had taken Deepti to the Barista near his place after spending the night with her, the way he used to...

My head jerked up as something hit the back of my neck. I turned around to see Rahul Kapoor throwing marigold flowers at me as he did his warm-up exercises. God, this guy was completely nuts. I turned back and started writing again – ignoring him was the only solution. He was just an attention-seeking dumbo. Of course, all actors thrived on attention, but – throwing flowers! How Hindi filmi could you get! Karan had once brought home hundreds of African daisies from a shoot and we'd... 'Cut. N.G.,' I told myself. I had to stop thinking about Karan. But why? Why shouldn't I enjoy thinking about him if I couldn't be with him? Because he was fucking around with that Deepti girl, that's why.

'Action!' Jumbo called out.

'How dare you!' Mrignayani said to the kulfiwala and slapped him. He pushed her and she fell on the street, her golden yellow ghagra riding up to her thighs.

'Cut! OK! That was brilliant, Monu,' Jumbo declared and turned to me. 'Now, what's the next shot we can take from this angle, Paro?'

I rifled through the pages in my hand. 'Long shot of Rahul Kapoor breaking the ice-slabs, Jumboji.'

Rahul stood behind the slabs of ice and practised his moves. Bare-chested. Nice body, I noted. Lithe and sinewy. Glistening with sweat. Or was it water sprayed on for effect?

'See if you can break the slabs,' Abbasbhai, the fight master, instructed.

'Yaaa...!' Rahul yelled as he broke the slabs of ice with a karate chop.

Mrignayani started clapping. I would also have been impressed if I hadn't supervised the art direction guys cutting each slab till just below the surface.

'That was mind-blowing,' Jumbo said encouragingly. He believed that his main job as a director was to be a one-man audience for his actors. His praise was always generous, while his criticism was of a gentle, 'I know you can do better' variety.

'Ya, but...' Rahul stepped back, scratching his head. 'I still don't feel convinced about my character being shirtless in this scene. I mean, this is a marketplace. Everybody else is fully clothed. How come I'm the only one who's shirtless?'

I remembered the first time I had seen Karan bare-chested. He'd insisted that I unbutton his shirt. I'd felt so shy, but I'd... Cut. Cut. Cut. Thoroughly N.G.

'You think too much,' Jumbo was saying, pinching Rahul's arm. 'Look at your body, look at your muscles. They look so good!'

Rahul rubbed his arm where Jumbo had pinched him, mumbling self-consciously, 'I've been working out in the gym, but my biceps really aren't big enough as yet.'

'That's it, that's what is so nice. Your muscles don't look put-on. They belong to a strong man, to a man who works in the fields,' Jumbo argued. 'I don't want a he-man bodybuilder.'

'But Jumboji, my character, he's from the city. How can he walk around on the streets bare-chested like a farmer?' Rahul hadn't given up. 'I don't mind showing my body, but it should be appropriate for the scene.'

'It's hot, you're sleeping, without a shirt, you're hearing some fight sounds, you're coming to investigate, what is your problem, huh?' Abbasbhai, the fight master, said irritably, flexing his muscles. He had reason enough to be bugged even otherwise. The director was supposed to hand over the shooting to the fight master for action scenes, but Jumbo was so much in his element directing maar-dhaad, Abbasbhai had been relegated to the sidelines.

'I don't mind exposing if the script demands it,' Munshiji, who was sitting near me, said in a girlish voice under his breath.

I made myself smile back at him. What if Karan married this Deepti and they had a baby together... Cut. N.G. What was the point of torturing myself this way?

'Why don't we put him in a thin white shirt,' Mrignayani said coyly, putting her hand on Jumbo's shoulder, 'and pour some water on him?'

So that's what we did.

When Mehboob Khan walked in and saw Rahul Kapoor
in the clinging wet shirt, he felt upstaged and tore his own
kurta to show his chest.

'What about the continuity?' I whispered to Jumbo.
'We've already shot half the scene with Mehboob wearing
a proper kurta.'

'What an idea, Mehboob!' Jumbo declared. 'You've got
such a powerful chest. We'll show your kurta being torn
in the shot. Got to think of costume continuity also, no?
Otherwise, this Paro here will eat my head.'

I'd been trying to maintain the costume continuity as
properly as I could. The continuity of the set had gone to
the dogs, but there wasn't much I could do about it. The
pine trees were supposed to be replaced after they dried
up. But the production manager hadn't been able to get that
many pine trees, so we had substituted mango and neem.

The camera rolled. Mehboob Khan punched the fighter,
who grabbed his kurta and pulled. The kurta tore, exposing
Mehboob's chest, and Jumbo called out happily, 'Cut. OK.'

'N.G.,' the superstar declared. 'You can't see my abs.
I've been doing three hundred sit-ups every day – my six-
pack should show.'

So we did another take. And another. And another. Till
the kurtas ran out.

'Hey, somebody get me some chai,' Jumbo said,
slumping tiredly into his chair as Mehboob Khan strode
back to his air-conditioned make-up van.

The production office was hidden behind the Tehelka
Barber Shop façade. I sneaked in during tea break and

smiled at the production manager. 'I need to make a local call, please.'

He opened the lock on the phone and pushed it towards me.

'Private call, please,' I smiled at him. He smiled back, pleasantly. Then he got it, smiled even more widely and left the room.

I dialled the number furiously.

'Good afternoon. Bose Productions,' the well-modulated voice said.

'Can I speak to Sharmishtha, please?'

Sharmishtha seemed very happy to be hearing from me.

'Hiii! Paro, after such a long time! How are you? What are you doing nowadays?'

'I'm working as an assistant director on a Hindi film.'

'You mean a running-around-the-trees Hindi film?'

'Ya, ya, a proper commercial Hindi film.'

'What's it like? I've been meaning to call you...'

'Actually,' I cut in abruptly, 'I called to ask about Karan. I saw him yesterday with Deepti Chawla – you know, that girl who works in Blue Moon agency,' I hurried on, before I lost my nerve. 'I wanted to ask you – was Karan having affairs behind my back?'

There was silence at the other end of the line. We'd got along well while working together in Mr Bose's office, but Sharmishtha wasn't a close friend. What would she think? She'd probably tell everybody, but what the heck, everybody knew everything anyway. Let them have one more laugh on me.

'I... I don't know what to say,' she mumbled.

'Please tell me. The truth would help.' I held my breath while I heard her brains creaking in the background. Maybe Karan hadn't been playing around. Or maybe she wouldn't tell me. How would knowing help, why the fuck did I have to…

'Yes he was. With a lot of girls, actually. I think with Deepti also, but I'm not quite sure when their affair started. Raghu says around Christmas, but I don't know. Actually, I don't really *know* anything about anything. It's just gossip, you know…'

I managed to say bye to her and get out of the office. The production manager gave me a wide smile and I was trying to smile back when suddenly, I felt ice sliding down my back.

I turned around in a fury.

'You bloody fucking sonofabitch,' I screamed at Rahul Kapoor. 'How dare you? How fucking dare you? You think that just because you are a bloody fucking star and I'm just an assistant director, you can behave any bloody way you like?'

I was shaking with rage. Rahul Kapoor was gaping at me, incredulous, the chunks of ice in his raised hand dripping water. I looked around, suddenly self-conscious. Everybody else was also staring at me, shocked.

I closed my eyes for a moment, then walked off, into the Costume Room.

I pulled off my hair-clip and then tied my hair even more tightly. I'd got a bad headache. I blinked a couple of times, waiting for my eyes to adjust to the dim light inside.

Take Two and Bihari were considerate enough to leave the Costume Room when Manoj came in and started shouting at me. My head was aching so badly, I could barely hear what Manoj was saying. But the gist was clear – if I ever stepped out of my bounds again, I'd be sacked.

After Manoj left, I sat down on a tin trunk, trying to massage my eyes with my trembling fingers. I remembered that Saira had given me a couple of cigarettes the day before. I fished around in my bag and found a broken one, with tobacco spilling out. I was searching for matches, when Rahul Kapoor walked into the Costume Room.

I was so mad, I could have hit him. He started chatting as usual, wandering around, wiping his hair with a towel. I was crumpling the unlit cigarette in my hand, watching the tobacco spill out, when he touched the edge of my dupatta.

'Rahulji,' I said, cutting him off in mid-sentence. I could feel the anger seething in me, but I was determined to be polite. I didn't want to lose my job because of this idiot. I would be so fucking polite...

'Rahulji,' I said, 'I'm extremely sorry about shouting at you right now in front of the whole unit.'

'Where's this "ji" business come from, hmm?' he said, taking my jooda pin out of his pocket and twirling it .

'Furthermore, I request you to kindly leave me alone. I'm saying this very nicely and politely, but I mean it.'

'What's got into you, baba?' he said, stringing his towel around his neck and sitting by my side. 'I heard that Manoj gave you a firing because you were rude to me, but I'll clear that up with him. The last thing I mind in the world is your being rude to me.'

I had to laugh at that. It wasn't a very humorous laugh, I was too close to tears for that. I held my head in my hands, trying to figure out some way of getting through to him.

'Of course,' he was saying, 'I'd prefer it if you were sweet and...'

'If you don't stop, I'll have to resign.'

'Arre yaar, don't...'

'Would you please, please, leave me alone?' I said.

'Look, I've just been teasing you and flirting with you till now, but I really do like...'

'Please,' I said, looking at him steadily.

He opened his mouth to say something, then just stood up and left.

I was so sick of waiting for the bus, I got up and started walking towards the Film City Gate. It was eight-thirty in the evening and quite dark, but tonight I wasn't bothered about the leopards, if at all there were any.

'Madam, don't walk alone in the dark,' Take Two called out after me.

'Nothing'll happen,' I said without turning around and kept on walking.

My cheeks hurt, but I refused to cry. I'd cried enough for Karan, that bloody fucking son of a bitch. Why should I drag his mother into this, she was probably just a sweet old woman.... I'd daydreamed of Karan taking me home to meet her. I'd be wearing my light yellow saree and I'd touch her feet... Shit! I was crying again. Why the fuck did I have to be such an...

'I'm really, really sorry,' Rahul Kapoor said.

I stopped short and hurriedly wiped away my tears. I hadn't realised that he'd been following me.

'I had no idea that my teasing upset you so much,' he said.

'I wasn't crying about you.' I had to be honest. Rahul Kapoor was just an irritant, he wasn't responsible for my tears. 'I was crying about my boyfriend... my ex-boyfriend.'

'Had a fight?' he asked gently.

'No, we've broken up,' I said shortly, starting to walk again. Why the fuck did I have to tell him this? Did I want a Mr Bose, take two?

'Are there really any leopards in Film City?' I wanted to change the subject.

'It's very rare, but once in a while a leopard wanders in from the Borivali National Park.'

'Oh, I thought that the guys were just pulling my leg because I'm new.'

'Look,' Rahul said, pointing. 'You can see the boundary wall of the national park from here.'

I strained my eyes, and I could make out a very tall wall in the far distance, marking the edge of the grassland.

'Have you ever been to the park?' he said.

'No.'

'It's a beautiful place,' Rahul said. 'You can hardly imagine that right in the middle of a congested city like Bombay, there's an eighty-seven square kilometre jungle. I haven't seen any leopards there, but I once saw this really beautiful flock of deer.'

'Oh really,' I said. Why was he walking with me? 'You're not driving today?'

'My jeep wouldn't start.'

'Why do you drive such a khatara jeep, anyway?'

'It's not a khatara,' he said, offended. 'It's a 1942 Ford. It's just got some starting problems.'

1942? It was a wonder that it ran at all, but I said, trying to be conciliatory, 'It does look very different from all those flashy cars on our set.'

'It's so cute-looking, na?' he said enthusiastically. 'I was really lucky. I got it for just forty thousand, but I wouldn't sell it for forty lakhs. It's got personality, character. People turn around to look at it on the street. And except for the fact that it doesn't start sometimes, it's so convenient. Do you know, its turning circle is less than a Santro's... Hello, what happened?'

I'd lagged behind, looking at the huge set of Goa by the roadside.

'No, nothing,' I said, catching up with him. 'I'm sorry. Ya, you were saying...'

'Have you ever seen the set from inside?'

I shook my head. I passed it everyday in the bus and I'd always wanted to, but there was never any time.

'Let's take a look,' he said.

'I'd love to, but will they allow us and all, I don't know.'

'Let's find out,' he said, and went and asked the guard.

The set was deserted, but the streetlights were on, so it felt like we were walking through a Goan marketplace in the late evening. Colourful sarongs and 'I love Goa' T-shirts hung up in roadside stalls were fluttering in the breeze. Hammocks were slung outside cafes, beside boards that

read, 'Happy Hours – 4 to 7 p.m.' All that was missing was
the laughter and bustle of people. Almost without realising
it, we started walking more slowly.

We crossed a stream on a small wooden bridge and I
stopped there for a moment, leaning on the railing. I closed
my eyes and I was in Goa. It was warm and sunny and I was
laughing because Karan was licking off the candyfloss that
had stuck to my face. A couple of passers-by were staring
at us, but we couldn't care less because…

'Do you know, it cost more than one and a half crore
rupees to make this set?' Rahul said.

'Oh, really?' I replied automatically. I had to stop
thinking about Karan. Had to make a determined effort. I
wasn't going to be a tragedy queen, I'd fucking survive this.

I forced myself to take interest in the Portuguese-style
verandahs which Rahul found so pretty, he wanted to have
them constructed on our set.

'Portuguese verandahs in a North Indian hill station?'
I said doubtfully.

'Who's bothered about authenticity in Jumboji's unit?'
he laughed, hopping into a hammock. 'As long as it looks
good, nobody cares. Hey, let's go and take a look at the
lighthouse.'

The picture-perfect red and white lighthouse was
constructed on a small hill at the edge of the set. By the
time we reached it, I was a little out of breath. But I was
in such a determinedly cheerful mood that when I walked
around and saw the ladders that went right up to the top,
I said, 'Let's climb up.'

I started climbing up the uneven wooden ladder, then realised midway that Rahul could probably see up my skirt.

'You go up first,' I said on the first landing.

He grinned, and climbed up the ladder with ease, solicitously turning around to help me over the difficult portions. The bamboo ladders didn't just have bad finishing, they also seemed a bit unstable, and by the time I reached the top, I was wondering why I'd ever had this bright idea of climbing up.

But the view changed my mind. The sleepy little Goan village was surrounded by miles of grassland, with just the tip of our hill station set visible about a kilometre away, looking incongruous but pretty. To our left, Rahul's Borivali National Park stretched as far as I could see. And a perfectly round moon hung above it all like a picture in a storybook.

'Oh, I didn't know that tonight was a full moon night!' I said with a smile. 'The stars never look very bright in Bombay because of the pollution, but the moon looks pretty anywhere.'

'What's your star sign?' Rahul asked. 'Mine's Sagittarius.'

'I don't believe in star signs. They're all bullshit.'

I remembered a time when Linda Goodman's *Love Signs* was a bible. Karan and I were supposed to be a good match. The discrepancies were explained away as 'Aquarius' independent nature cannot understand Cancer's need for reassurance,' while in real life, he was just fucking around behind my back.

'Cut! N.G.!' I told myself angrily. What was the point of it all, to just keep on torturing myself, when Karan was out around town, having fun with that Deepti girl? He was probably living it up in discos and pubs, dancing and drinking, and I didn't know what else – actually I did know what else – while I went to bed hungry, weeping, thinking of him...

'Will you have dinner with me tonight?'

Rahul stared at me in surprise, then said, 'Of course I will.'

I turned and started climbing down the ladder. Two could play at a game, couldn't they? Why should I remain the poor, wronged woman, long suffering, more sinned against than sinning? I'd beat them at their own game, the fucking bastards...

'This is just a one-off, OK?' I said to him abruptly.

'OK, OK,' he said quickly. Then, 'What is a... "one-off"?'

'One-of-a-kind,' I explained. 'Like in ads, some are a series with common characters or a common concept, like, say, the Rin ads, you know?'

'Ya, ya.'

'And then you have one-of-a-kinds where there's only one ad based on a certain concept.'

'Oh, OK, I get it, ya, ya, sure, sure,' he said quickly.

I climbed down, ignoring the helping hand he held out to me. I was quite capable of climbing down unwieldy ladders all by myself, thank you. And I didn't want him to get any ideas.

SEVEN

'Where are you from?' I said, since I had to say
something. I had no idea what I could converse about with
Rahul Kapoor, but we were sitting across a table in a posh,
air-conditioned restaurant and after we'd placed our orders,
I presumed that some kind of conversation was supposed
to take place.

'New Delhi,' he said.

Karan was also from Delhi. Cut. N.G. What was the
point of going out with somebody else if I kept on thinking
about Karan? And anyway, what was the big deal about
being from Delhi? Lots of people were. Even Saira was
from Delhi.

'Are you related to the Kapoors?' I ploughed on with
the conversation. 'To Raj Kapoor?'

'No, no, not at all. None of my relatives belong to the
Hindi film industry.' Then he added sheepishly, 'Actually
my real surname is Bhanot. I changed it to Kapoor when
I came to Bombay because there are so many Kapoors in
the industry. It sounds more like hero material, no?'

'I guess,' I said wryly. 'Did your father mind your changing your name?'

'What does he *not* mind? He minds my coming to Bombay, he minds my not finishing my graduation, he minds my acting in Hindi films. Especially the Hindi films bit.'

I nodded. If I had a son who left his studies to come to Bombay and act in Jumbo's films, I would mind.

'He's stopped speaking to me since he saw *Maut Ke Sikandar*.' Rahul sighed, shook his head and told me, 'He teaches English literature at Jawaharlal Nehru University.'

'Oh, that's the place where there's all this radical left stuff happening, na?'

'Not so much nowadays. Things are changing everywhere. Papa's a hardcore Marxist, though. Completely intellectual. We're Punjabi, but he only watches films by Bengali neorealist directors. Bimal Roy's his favourite.'

'Oh, I love Bimal Roy's films. Especially *Bandini*. Have you seen it?'

'At least twenty times. We had a video cassette at home,' Rahul said enthusiastically. 'But his *Do Bigha Zameen* is a far better film, actually. It's much more understated.'

'Understated, hmm.' I looked at him quizzically. 'What are you doing here – in Jumbo's films?'

'Oh, I love commercial Hindi films. Really I do. From the bottom of my heart. Realistic art films are fine, but they leave you feeling depressed. There's enough in most people's lives that gets them down, why should a man go to a theatre and feel even more miserable?'

'I think that *I* would feel quite miserable if I had to watch Jumbo's film for three hours in a movie theatre,' I said dryly. 'I much prefer old Hindi films.'

Karan liked Hollywood films, especially sci-fi and... Cut. N.G.

'But there are thousands, no, lakhs of people out there who spend their hard-earned money to go and see Jumboji's films,' Rahul was saying enthusiastically. 'A rickshaw-wala who earns forty rupees a day pays twenty rupees to sit in a theatre in the evening and watch Jumboji's film. And he says paisa vasool at the end of it.'

'But you're not a rickshaw-wala. Don't your sensibilities get offended by the inane dialogues and loud costumes?' I said. 'You usually wear a white shirt and blue jeans when you come on the set. I'm sure you don't like the costumes you have to wear.'

'Oh, you've noticed my clothes,' he said, quite pleased.

'No, no, it's just that I've been taking care of costumes and continuity, so I notice people's clothes more,' I said quickly, then regretted it. It sounded too defensive.

'I don't dislike the costumes, actually. They're dramatic, larger than life. Everything about Hindi films is larger than life. That's the style, the way the narrative structure works.'

'"Narrative structure" and all! Does your father say that?'

'What does my father have to do with this?' he said, frowning.

He looked very intense, and I suddenly realised that he was attractive. I mean, I'd always known that he was handsome, but it'd had nothing to do with me. Like the verandah of Mehboob Khan's house on the set, or the façade of the church, his looks gave production value to the film.

'No, I just thought, since he teaches English Literature at Jawaharlal Nehru University and all...' I said, my hands toying with the red rose on our table.

'I'm not quoting his ideas,' he said huffily. Then relaxed. 'But you're right, I must have picked up some of this jargon from Papa.'

'Which subject were you studying in college?' I said, plucking a petal from the rose and nibbling it. 'You mentioned that you didn't finish your graduation...'

'Are you very hungry?' he said, disconcerted.

'What? Oh, no. Rose petals are supposed to be very good for the eyes,' I said, offering him a petal. He took it a little hesitantly and ate it.

'Hey, it's not bad,' he said enthusiastically, plucking all the petals off the rose and giving me half of them.

I stole a sidelong glance at the people sitting at the other tables, hoping that nobody had noticed us.

'You were talking about Hindi films,' I said with a quick smile, stuffing the rose petals into my purse.

'Let's forget about intellectual justifications for why Hindi films are the way they are – the proof of the pudding is in the eating. I was so crazy about movies when I was a kid, that I once stood in a line for five hours to get a ticket for *Sholay*,' he told me. 'I know most of its dialogues by heart. What I wouldn't do to get Dharamendra's role in a film like that! "Basanti bhi tayyar, Mausi bhi tayyar. Is liye marna cancel."'

'Dharamendra's cute, but I liked Amitabh more in the film,' I said. 'He's so cool.'

'Oh, he's brilliant,' Rahul said, eyes sparkling. '"Arre, Basanti se uski shaadi kar ke to dekhiye, ye juwe aur sharaab ki aadat to do din mein chhoot jaayegi."'

'"Arre beta, mujh budhiya ko samjha rahe ho,"' I grinned back. '"Yeh sharaab aur juwe ki aadat kisi ki chhooti hai aaj tak?"'

'"Mausi, aap Veeru ko nahi jaanti. Vishwas keejiye, woh is tarah ka insaan nahi hai,"' Rahul said, delighted. '"Ek baar shaadi ho gayi to woh us gaanewali ke ghar jaana band kar dega, sharaab apne aap chhoot jaayegi."'

'Actually, I loved Amitabh's romance with Jaya Bhaduri,' I said, laughing. 'He's quiet, but so romantic, so intense.'

'You like the strong, silent type, huh?' Rahul said. 'No problem, I can also keep quiet.'

He stared deep into my eyes.

If you can't beat them, join them. 'Let's see who blinks first,' I said flippantly.

We locked eyes over the table. He was trying so hard to look at me seductively, I smiled, but I didn't blink. He was welcome to think of it as a romantic gesture, there was no way I was going to let him win. Karan had told me once that lovers looked into each other's eyes to subconsciously check out whether the pupils were dilated because of sexual excitement. Hmm, Rahul's pupils definitely were dilated, the black almost crowding out the reddish-brown iris. It struck me that perhaps my pupils were getting dilated as well, and I looked away immediately.

'You blinked first,' he shouted triumphantly.

'I did not,' I said, irritated, looking back at him. 'I just looked away, I didn't blink. See, my eyes are still open. I haven't blinked till now.'

'I haven't blinked either,' he said.

'You're lying, I saw you blink when...' I shut up. This was ridiculous. We were squabbling like kids. How would Kavita and Saira analyse this?

'You're a bad loser,' he said.

I gave him a calm 'You're such a kid' smile.

'What?' he said.

'You were supposed to be proving to me that you can do the strong silent type number,' I said.

He gave me a sheepish smile and said, 'Let's do a second take.'

'No second takes in life,' I said, digging into the steaming plate of spaghetti the waiter had served me. 'You get only one chance.'

He rolled his spaghetti on his fork, then looked up at me and said, 'I know one shouldn't look a gift horse in the mouth, but how did you agree to go out with me?'

'Oh, I came out with you only because I didn't feel like going back to my place and eating milk powder with cornflakes and water. That's what I have most nights for dinner. And for breakfast, of course,' I told him.

He looked at me for a moment like I'd lost it, or something.

'How can you eat milk powder with cornflakes and water?'

'How can you eat them without water?' I said.

He shook his head.

'What about you?' I said. 'Do you cook?'

'Sure, I cook. Come and live with me. I'll serve you breakfast in bed every morning. And when you come back at night, I'll keep dinner ready. With candlelight and wine. Which wine do you like?'

There he went again. I'd thought, for a change, he's not flirting with me. Anyway, what was the harm with flirting just for tonight, I'd come out on a date with him.

'I like champagne. And I prefer moonlight.'

'Ye shyam mastani...' Rahul sang along with Kishore Kumar on Radio Mirchi and turned to give me a smile.

I smiled back, but I was starting to feel a little tense. Did he expect the evening to end with a kiss? I'd flirted a bit with him and – what was it that Suresh had said to Saira after he'd grabbed her and kissed her – 'Only nerds ask.' And of course, Mr Bose. How could I have forgotten about him?

Rahul's hand brushed my thigh lightly as he changed gear. I crossed my legs and gave him a look out of the corner of my eyes. Maybe it wasn't such a bad idea to kiss him. He had very sensuous-looking lips – dark and full, with a well-shaped cupid's whatchamacallit. Actually, I didn't know whether it felt any better to kiss nice-looking lips. I reminded myself to ask Saira. The only guy I'd ever kissed was Karan. It would serve him right if I went and kissed Rahul Kapoor. Not that he'd care, though. That Deepti girl was much fairer than me and she'd got pink... Cut. N.G.

The jeep stopped at a light and as Rahul turned to me, I blurted out, 'You might be thinking that just because I went out with you, I'll let you kiss me. But I'm not.'

That was extremely badly put, but at least I'd said it. In advance.

He raised his eyebrows. 'The thought hadn't even crossed my mind.'

Liar, I thought, but I felt very silly.

The next morning, he greeted me with a brilliant smile when he came on the set. I smiled back, politely, but a bit frostily. Frost was necessary, I'd realised, thinking it over in bed. Otherwise he'd feel free to take liberties with me, now that I'd gone out with him once.

The brilliance of his smile dimmed a bit. He looked at me enquiringly. I shrugged. He shrugged back and looked away. Message Received. Good.

We had an early pack-up that day and I was enjoying the sunset as I walked to the Film City gate, swinging my bag, when I realised that Rahul was nonchalantly walking by my side. I looked at him, too exasperated to say anything.

'My jeep broke down. Again.'

Sure. The same way it wouldn't start yesterday when he'd wanted to walk with me and had been coaxed into life after I'd asked him out.

'Look, I'd said to you, very clearly, hadn't I – just a one-off – don't you understand?' I said.

'"One-off", of course I understand, not like the Rin ads.' There was a pause as we walked together and then he said quietly, 'But why? Why just a one-of-a-kind, why not a series, like the Rin ads?'

I wondered how to reply, then decided to be straightforward. The last thing I wanted to do was to lead him on.

'Look,' I said, 'to be truthful, my going out with you didn't have much to do with you, as such. Means, I went out with you because I saw my ex-boyfriend with some girl. I could just as well have gone out with Manoj or Kapil or… or anybody.'

We walked together in silence for a while. I hoped that he wasn't feeling bad, but even more than that, I hoped that the score was clear.

'By the way,' I said, 'can I have my jooda pin back?'

He took it out of his pocket, twirled it a couple of times, making the bells tinkle, and then handed it to me.

'I'd grown a bit fond of it,' he said.

I wanted to frown, but I couldn't help smiling. The weather was much too pleasant. I stopped to tie my hair into a knot with my jooda pin. It felt nice to have my pin back.

'Tell me something,' he said abruptly. 'Don't you find me attractive?'

'No,' I said, but since I didn't particularly want to do a hatchet job on his ego, I added, 'Obviously you're very good-looking and all, but you're not my types.'

'Types, means like…'

'Means like… I go for dark guys and you're fair.' Karan was very dark, and I'd fallen for him at first sight.

'No problem,' Rahul said confidently. 'Kryolan Pancake, Shade No. 626 E.'

I smiled, and shook my head.

'Aren't you ever going to give up trying?' I said.

'Of course I will. Very soon. As soon as you say yes.'

'Ooh, like that! You're going to be interested only till I'm hard-to-get. As soon as you get me...'

'I don't want to get you, Paro,' he said, suddenly turning serious. 'I don't know why, but my heart feels drawn...'

'Save these dialogues for the screen.'

'OK.' He made a face, then switched back to being non-serious. 'So tell me, what else is your type – what kind of guys do you go for?'

What kind of guys *did* I go for? Oh yes, of course. Kavita's patterns.

'You know, I've got this pattern of falling for all the wrong kind of guys. And of having these really fucked-up kind of relationships,' I said. 'I mean, if you're like, Prince Charming, I'm obviously not going to fall for you.'

'So... What do I have to do, to qualify?'

'Well, get married, for starters.'

'My God!' Pause. 'Won't having another girlfriend do?'

'No,' I said. 'I'm the old-fashioned types.'

EIGHT

Mrignayani ran down the dimly lit street, hotly pursued by four burly men. She stumbled over a stone and fell. The men surrounded her, laughing loudly, as she clutched her dupatta to her heaving bosom.

'Ha, ha, ha,' the villain leered, revealing a mouthful of golden teeth. 'Which one of your two-two lovers has drunk so much of his mother's milk that he can dare to save you from the biggest...'

The men whirled around as Rahul Kapoor scaled over a fence on a white horse and – all the lights on the set went off.

'What the fuck is going on?' Mrignayani demanded shrilly. 'This is the third time the generator has conked out tonight. What kind of shooting is this? Where's the production manager?'

I sighed and closed the continuity book. It would take half an hour for them to repair the generator. If we were lucky.

'Tea break,' Jumbo announced.

The last two times the lights had gone off, I'd been bumped into by four assorted men, so I retreated into a nearby patch of trees. Real trees, that'd had nothing to do with the art direction department. I found a log to sit on and flexed my feet, feeling glad for the rest. The way things were going, the shooting seemed set to go on till morning.

All the other assistant directors cribbed about the night shoots, but I preferred them. I said that it was because we didn't have to stand in the sun all day long. But the real reason was that the work distracted me from the temptation of calling up Karan.

It was two weeks since I had seen him with Deepti and I hadn't called him since then. What was the badge that Saira's boyfriend had got from Narcotics Anonymous after he had stopped using drugs for two weeks? 'Clean and Serene for 14 Days'. I hadn't been serene, but yes, I had been able to keep myself from making blank calls to Karan for the last fourteen nights. Even if he called me up now and called me over, I wouldn't go. I hoped that I wouldn't go. But what if he really...

Rahul Kapoor took my hand in his and sat down by my side.

'What...' I jerked my hand away but he held on.

'Hey, hey, relax. I'm just reading your hand.' He shone a torch on my palm and looked at it contemplatively. 'Good strong life line,' he told me. 'You'll live to be ninety-seven.'

It was so Hindi-filmi romantic, I couldn't help smiling. Midnight, the two of us sitting on a log. Beneath mango trees that rustled in the breeze. And him reading my hand. With a torch!

As it is, Rahul Kapoor's ideas about wooing definitely were inspired by Hindi films. He'd sing love songs to me. And dance to them. He'd get me boxes of candy and flowers. With my sweet tooth, I didn't mind the chocolates, but I did admonish him when he plucked flowers from the set and presented them to me – it took us a lot of effort to tend to those plants.

'You'll have two boys and... one girl. Yes.'

Did that include the baby I hadn't had?

'What about work?' I said, trying to distract myself.

'Your career will really take off when you're about twenty-seven,' he informed me. 'But you won't be making a great deal of money till you're... thirty-one.'

I looked at him compassionately. He was trying his best to charm me, but his style was hampered a little by the fact that he was wearing a bright pink chiffon shirt with purple silk pants. Sometimes I felt so old, I wished for his sake that he were trying these lines on someone else.

'And when will I get married?' I asked him tiredly.

'In about... uh, how old are you?'

'Twenty-two,' I said. I wasn't really lying – I was just two months away from my twenty-second birthday.

'I'm twenty,' he said brightly. 'Doesn't matter, I don't care about such things. How do they make a difference, huh? Na umraki seema ho, na janam ka ho bandhan... So you will get married when you are...' He bent my hand and pressed the skin so that the lines became more prominent. 'When you are twenty-six years and seven months old.'

'How many days?' I asked dryly.

'Seven days. Hmm now, let's see, nice long fingers. You're an artist.'

'Wow!'

'Strong will power,' he said, pressing my thumb back. 'But a bit stubborn. OK, now curl your hand into a tight fist. Right, ya, tighter. Now, relax.'

He tried to open my fist. I resisted.

'Hey, I said relax.'

I shrugged and slowly let him open my hand till his palm was lying flat on mine.

'You didn't let me open your hand in the beginning, and even when you did, you opened it very slowly – that shows that you don't trust easily,' he said. 'You're too closed as a person. Open up, you'll enjoy life more.'

I took my hand back from him and lit a cigarette.

'Do you know what "trust me" means in Polish?' I asked.

He shook his head.

'What?'

'"Fuck you."'

He laughed. I smiled.

'So, when a guy says "trust me",' I said to him, 'a warning bell rings in my head.'

He made a face. 'Why are you so hard, so defensive?'

'Have to be, living in Bombay, alone.'

He was silent for a while, but only for a while.

'But what about love? Don't you believe in love?'

'Men give love in order to get sex. Women give sex in order to get love.' I'd read that somewhere, or maybe Saira had told me.

'Baap re, you're very unromantic.'

'You know something, all those stupid, stupid fairy tales and love songs which we've been hearing right from the time when we were, like, toddlers – they are what fuck us up. Life's not a bloody Mills and Boon romance. Not by far. Happily ever after never happens.'

'It does, too. I've even got a white horse. I'll take you on it and ride into the sunset....'

'Bah!' I said, taking the torch from his hand. I would have got up and walked off, but my feet were hurting too much. I propped up my continuity book between us and turned the torch to face it, so that we were lit by a more even, diffused light.

'What's your favourite fairy tale?' I said, trying to change the subject.

'Sleeping Beauty,' he said. And grinned. 'What about yours?'

'Dhruv Tara. Do you know it?'

He shook his head.

'Do you know who Dhruv Tara is?'

He shook his head again.

I made a face and looked up at the sky.

'Hey, it's not *so* bad,' he said.

I pointed to the North Star.

'Between those branches, there, that's Dhruv Tara.'

'Oh. I never knew,' he said.

'Ya, ya, angrez da puttar.'

'So, what's his story?'

'Well, it's a bit longish-types. You won't get bored?'

'Zyada bhav mat kha. Bol,' he said. Then, more softly, 'No, I won't get bored.'

'Once upon a time, long, long ago, there lived a king who had two wives,' I began. 'The one he liked, his aavadti, his favourite queen, stayed with him in the palace. And the naavadti – how does one say it – the one who was, yes, out of favour, she stayed in a hut in the forest, with her son, Dhruv. One day, when Dhruv was seven years old, he told his mother that he wanted to go to the palace and meet his father. She was reluctant, but he insisted, so she dressed him up in the best clothes he had, and sent him off.

'Dhruv went to the palace and his father was very happy to see him. He made Dhruv sit on his lap and gave him sweets to eat. But when the king's favourite queen and her children came along, she made Dhruv get off his father's lap so that her children could sit there.

'Dhruv went back home to his mother, crying bitterly. She told him that the only one who could get him his rightful place was Bhagwan Vishnu. So Dhruv went deep into the forest and meditated for many years. He didn't sleep, didn't eat, didn't even drink any water. The gods were moved by this small child's tapasya, and Bhagwan Vishnu appeared in front of Dhruv to ask him what he wanted. Dhruv said that he wanted a place from where nobody could ever move him. That's how he became Dhruv Tara – the North Star.

'Everything else moves – the earth moves, the sun moves, even the stars move, but Dhruv Tara remains constant, unchanging. Nobody can ever move him from his place.'

'That's cool,' Rahul said, 'but he must be getting lonely up there. Nobody to talk to, nobody to flirt with, nobody to love.'

'Flirting! That's all you can think of,' I said, irritated, and got up.

'Close the door quickly. Quickly, quickly. Yes,' Saira giggled, depositing the tray with tea and freshly-fried finger chips on the bed. 'Bolt the door. Right. Now we're safe.'

Kavita and I attacked the chips gleefully. Saira's landlady had a strict 'No Cooking Allowed' rule, but she was sleeping right now, so we'd carried off this coup.

'Why are all landladies so grouchy?' I asked, choosing one orange-pink and one shocking pink cushion to lean back on. Once, in a wild burst of inspiration, Saira had blown up her pay decorating her tiny room in shades of pink. She'd been ecstatic about it for three weeks. And then it had started getting on her nerves. She now wanted to do up her room in light blue, but that had to wait for at least six months, since she was currently broke.

'Maybe someday we'll own houses in Bombay,' Saira said, 'and we'll be very mean to our paying guests.'

'No male visitors,' Kavita said like a school-marm.

'No talking to my husband. You need anything, talk only to me,' I said shrilly, imitating my landlady.

'No overnight visitors allowed except for mother, father, sisters and real brothers. Copy of ration card from hometown and current identity cards required as proof of "realness",' Saira giggled.

'Good God!' I said. 'Ration card as well? But if it's just a copy, I could design it on Adobe Photoshop.'

'Soaking clothes in a bucket for more than one week is not allowed,' Saira said.

'You are permitted to have male visitors in your room, but the door must be kept open and both pairs of feet must be on the ground at all times,' Kavita said grouchily.

'What?' I couldn't believe that one could be for real.

'No, seriously. I was staying in this Parsi lady's place. That's the time Abhijeet and I started going around. It didn't make much difference – we smooched in the balcony,' Kavita laughed. 'We used to have so much fun those days.'

'The more fun it is in the beginning, the nastier it gets in the end,' Saira said, suddenly becoming serious.

'What happened?' Kavita looked up at her.

'Nothing. Just like that,' Saira said, adjusting the cushion behind her. 'My grandmother used to say, "Don't laugh so much today, you'll have to cry tomorrow."'

'Zyada bhav mat kha, yaar,' I said.

'Nothing, baba,' Saira said, sipping her tea.

Kavita gestured to me with her eyes. I shrugged and started reading the magazine she was holding in her hands.

Saira being Saira, she couldn't hold it in any longer and burst out, 'I broke up with Whacko.'

'Why, what happened?' Kavita and I stopped pretending to be interested in the best way of removing chewing gum stuck on clothes.

'Whacko and me – we were supposed to be having an open relationship, na? That party we went to, on Saturday, for the music launch, I flirted with some guy. Whacko slapped me.'

'What? He *slapped* you?'

'In front of everybody?' Kavita asked, shocked.

'No, thank God for that. In the taxi, while coming home. I was teasing him, saying that other guy had much bigger biceps, and suddenly, out of the blue – phachack!'

'Did you slap him back?' Kavita said.

'Of course I did. Twice. Then I told the driver to stop and made Whacko get off.'

'My God, I just can't believe it,' I said. 'A *slap*, for God's sake!'

'I know,' Saira said, shaking her head. 'Sala, I'm not supposed to get angry when he calls up his ex-girlfriend. And he *hits* me when I flirt with some guy. None of my boyfriends has ever hit me. We were both of us very drunk, but still, it's crazy.'

'Whose idea was it in the first place – this "open relationship" business?' I asked.

'It was *his* idea,' Saira said indignantly.

'I always thought he's weird,' Kavita said. 'You can never tell with these creative types.'

'Hello?' I said.

'I didn't mean you,' Kavita said quickly.

'Anyway, I don't want to talk about him any more. He's out of my life. Finito,' Saira said. 'I went out with Chintu yesterday. He's such a darling. He's the one man who's always there whenever I need him.'

Chintu was Saira's childhood friend. He was short and fat and absolutely cuddly. He'd always been in love with

Saira, and she loved him too, but when they tried going around, she realised that she didn't find him sexually attractive. Now they were on a 'Let's stay good friends' level.

'Where did he take you?' Kavita asked.

'We went to Juhu Beach and I ate six plates of ragda patties,' Saira said.

'*Six* plates of ragda patties? But what about your diet?'

'I took a holiday from my diet. Just for yesterday,' Saira said.

'Have some chips,' I offered. 'They're delicious.'

'No, no, I've made them for just the two of you,' Saira said virtuously, sipping her tea. 'I'm glad to see you enjoying them.'

'Come on,' I said. 'Eating chips once is not going to make a difference to your weight. You'll feel better.'

'Cindy Crawford says that if you want to eat white bread, you might just as well sit on it, because that's where it's all going to end up. On your butt,' Saira said, more to herself than to anybody else. 'Chips are probably worse.'

I could imagine chip-like projections appearing on my thighs, and quickly smothered the thought.

'Who cares?' I said bravely. 'Why should we bother so much about looking good for guys? Do they take so much care of their looks for us?'

Saira couldn't take it any more and attacked the chips. 'You're right, why should we be so hyper about getting fat?' she said, her mouth full of finger chips. 'God, chips taste so much better than cucumbers.'

'I'm definitely in favour of Saira eating the chips. But, about what Paro was saying, men do work hard at becoming rich and successful because they know that's what attracts women,' Kavita said pragmatically.

'I was thinking, means, I wanted to ask you, like, you know...' Both Kavita and Saira were staring at me, so I went on, in a rush. 'Does it matter how a guy looks? I mean, does it actually feel nicer to kiss a guy who's got beautiful lips?'

'Why?' They pounced on me.

'No, no, no, nothing like that. I haven't kissed anybody yet, means I haven't kissed Rahul Kapoor. If I ever do, I'll tell you.'

Kavita rolled her eyes but didn't say anything.

'You better,' Saira muttered darkly, then perked up, spearing a couple of chips with her fork and munching them thoughtfully. 'Hmm, I've never really thought about that, you know. It's so automatic – you see sexy lips, you want to kiss them. But, ya, let me remember. The best kisser I've known is umm... Anand? Yes. Definitely. He was the second guy I ever kissed. He'd got, ya, he'd got thin lips, nothing special-looking, but the things he could do with his tongue...'

Saira froze. Somebody was knocking at the door. She hid the tray under her bed, we quickly chomped up whatever was in our mouths, and then she opened the door.

'Yes, Aunty?' Saira said sweetly.

'Phone call,' her landlady said dourly.

'Thank you, Aunty,' Saira said with a smile.

Her landlady didn't smile back, just looked at us suspiciously, pulling her dressing gown tightly around herself. She had a strong, humourless face, and I could imagine her inspecting a copy of Saira's 'brother's' current I-card and ration card from their hometown.

Saira said, 'Excuse me,' to us and closed the door behind herself when she left. Sometimes it surprised me – Saira was so irreverent most of the time but she had all these 'little niceties' intact.

'Come on, confess,' Kavita said. 'You like this actor.'

'No I don't. I was just *wondering*, that's all. Just because a thought enters your head, does it...'

Saira came in, looking very upset, and shut the door behind herself with a bang.

'Whacko had called. He wants to make up. I told him to fuck off and hung up on him.'

'That's good,' we told her.

'But I want to make up with him,' Saira said. And burst into tears.

Shweta was getting ready to go out when I got back to our room. I was glad – I'd be able to fall asleep in peace for a change. I lay in bed, watching her reflection in the mirror as she expertly outlined her lips with a maroon pencil. Just outside the natural lip-line of her upper lip since it was too thin. Just inside the natural lip-line of her lower lip, since that was too full. I wondered whether, below that tough Bombay-girl exterior of Shweta's, there was a person who'd also gone through...

'Have you ever had a heartbreak, Shweta?'

She looked up at me, surprised, as she applied her lipstick. Somehow, we'd never had a personal talk before.

'Of course I have. Everybody does sometime,' she said, closing the lipstick case. 'You know, the best way you can get over that guy is by finding another. Use a thorn to remove a thorn.'

'How do you know that I've had a heartbreak?' I'd never told her.

'Well, I can hear you crying into your pillow at night.'

As she applied mascara to her eyelashes, I wondered how to construe what she'd said. If it was out of sympathy, well, that was sweet of her, thank you. Or was it that my crying irritated her? It wasn't impossible. Oh well, what the hell, I also paid two thousand rupees a month for the room. If she was entitled to play her heavy metal music, I was entitled to cry into my pillow every night if I felt like.

'I love you,' Rahul said softly, looking deep into my eyes. 'I need you like my lungs need air to breathe, like my heart needs blood to pump, like... like... what comes next?'

'Like my tongue needs water,' I said, reading out from the sheet of dialogues.

'Right. Like my tongue needs water to drink, like my bones need calcium to stand tall, like...'

'Calcium and vitamin D,' I corrected, casting a quick glance at the trees above us, to check whether any of them was swaying too much. The art direction guys had created a grove of Gulmohar trees especially for this scene, and while they looked very pretty, I wouldn't have bet on the chances of none of them toppling over.

'Oh, vitamin D also?' he said and massaged his temples. He took a deep breath and tried to go on, but just couldn't.

'Bones need vitamin D,' he muttered to himself, then gently tapped Munshiji, the scriptwriter, who was sleeping in a chair near us. 'Sir, about my dialogues...'

'What about them?' Munshiji said crankily, rubbing his eyes.

'I'm not feeling convinced about them,' Rahul said.

'People talk poetically when they fall in love,' Munshiji snapped.

'Poetry... OK,' Rahul said diplomatically. 'But I was thinking about my characterisation. If my character were a doctor, then maybe he'd write poetry like this, but...'

'These dialogues lead to a song. Stop thinking about characterisation,' Munshiji snapped. 'And anyway, even schoolchildren know about all this science stuff nowadays.'

'Fine, but...' Rahul didn't give up easy.

'This kal ka chhokra is teaching *me* about characterisation. I'll tell you about characterisation,' Munshiji said, wagging his finger in Rahul's face. 'Young man, you weren't even born when I won my first Filmfare Award.'

Rahul slunk away, mumbling something about going over his lines again. But Munshiji wasn't through yet. He turned to me.

'These boys, they do theatre in Delhi and come here, they think they know acting. Always my character this, my character that. Tell me, in a film like this, nothing makes sense, how is this one boy's character supposed to make sense? Now you only tell me.'

I nodded obediently. Behind Munshiji's shoulder I could see Rahul talking to three girls who were asking him for his autograph. He gallantly offered them his chair but since the three girls couldn't fit into one chair, they all stood around giggling as he flashed his dimples at them. With the setting sun bathing him in back-light, he looked every inch the movie star – tall, fair, handsome. In fact, he was so conventionally good-looking, it would be too silly to feel attracted to him.

'Now, when I entered films, that, young lady, that was the golden era of Hindi films,' Munshiji reminisced. 'Dilip Kumar... Can any of these young idiots even compare with him? Do you know, I wrote my first screenplay for Dilip Kumar?'

I realised with a start that Munshiji was as old as my grandfather. My grandfather was a retired schoolteacher and his favourite pastimes were spinning khadi and singing Tukaram's devotional songs. He hadn't seen a Hindi film in years. The only thing he watched on television was the morning news on NDTV. I thought of my grandfather having to work in a place like this, and I felt a surge of sympathy for Munshiji.

'If you don't like these kinds of scripts, why are you writing them, sir?' I said hesitantly.

'Money! Money! Why else would anybody write something like this?' Munshiji shook his head and pressed his temples. 'My psychiatrist says that I should write at least one good script a year. That might reduce my depression.'

Oh! So it wasn't just depressing love lives that made people go to shrinks.

'But what is the point of writing a script which nobody'll make into a film?' Munshiji said. 'All that sells nowadays

is terrorists and marriage videos and lost-and-found. And
of course, the heroine shaking her ass. Everybody watches
that. I'm so bored with this romance business. But what can
I do?'

'But maybe you can… write a good script just for
yourself,' I suggested.

'What will I do with my "good script"? If I show it
around, it'll spoil my market. And at home… My wife fell
in love with me because of my writing, but that was a long
time ago. Nowadays she doesn't even want to listen to my
poems… Anyway, a script that isn't made into a film is like
a song without a voice to bring it alive, like a bride waiting
for a bridegroom who'll never come, like…' He stopped
suddenly and looked at me sadly. 'See, what will I write
now, all that comes into my head these days is clichéd.'

I wanted to reach out to him, but didn't know what to
say. He got up slowly and wandered off.

'Paro, where's Mrignayani's golden kamarbandh?' Manoj
called out to me. 'Isn't she supposed to be wearing it in
the song?'

On my way to the Costume Room, I paused when I saw
that Rahul had put his arm around one of the girls. What
the hell was he doing with his *arm* around…? He caught
me looking angrily at him and gleefully tossed his cap into
the air.

NINE

And then it was time for the buffalo song. Forty big, fat buffaloes descended on our set, mooing and shitting all over the place. They were lovingly washed, and groundnut oil was applied on their black hides and horns to make them look more photogenic.

'They should have had bigger horns,' Jumbo grumbled, getting sentimental. 'These Maharashtrian buffaloes are no comparison to our Bihari ones. We have such a beautiful seven-year-old buffalo back home. My mother makes ghee from her milk and sends it to us. I'll tell my wife to make gajar ka halwa with our ghee and bring it for all of you sometime. She doesn't make it as well as my mother does, but still...'

The one sorrow of Jumbo's life was that his mother didn't stay with him. She didn't feel comfortable in the posh, Japanese-style house which his wife had got done up by a professional interior designer. In fact, even Jumbo didn't feel comfortable there. He was most at home on the sets.

'Let the buffaloes graze behind the church,' Jumbo said kindly. 'We'll have them brought here when they're needed.'

'Are the buffaloes trained to perform for the camera?' I asked Manoj.

Manoj shot me a dirty look, which was a bit unfair, considering all that had happened on our set with animals. The Siamese cat which had been brought in to replace the monkey had scratched not just Rahul, but also Manoj and the other assistant, Kapil. Rahul was the only one who hadn't had to take a tetanus injection because he'd had one recently – for the monkey bite.

I checked Rahul's costume continuity. The song took off from the scene in which he'd proposed to Mrignayani, giving all those ajeebogareeb medical similes for his love. I looked him over from top to toe, making sure that his costume was the same. Red cap, golden yellow shirt with sleeves rolled up, belt had been a different shade of brown, but it wouldn't register because the buckle was similar, black leather pants, white shoes. OK. When I looked back up at his face, he was blushing. I laughed.

Rahul had a lot more blushing to do that day. Mrignayani was cool with the vigorous pelvic thrusts that she was required to do for the song picturisation, but he was maha embarrassed about it.

'Why are you sharmaoing like a girl?' the choreographer, Jojo, shouted at Rahul. 'Look at this Mrignayani, she's so bindaas. You're a man, man. Just do it. Yeah, right, like that.'

Rahul and Mrignayani were dancing in a small boat that was anchored in the middle of a thirty-foot wide pond that had been dug up at the bottom of the hill. Adding a rustic touch to the locale were three buffaloes floating in the pond and five munching grass around it.

The choreographer shouted out the beats. At one, Rahul and Mrignayani thrust their pelvises forward, in sync. At two, they bent backwards and shook their heads. At three, they held each other's hands and straightened up. At four, Rahul kissed Mrignayani's cheek while she fluttered her eyelashes. Ten pairs of dancers standing on the side of the pond mirrored their actions. One, two, three, four. One, two, three, four. The only variation being that Rahul kissed her right cheek first and then her left cheek.

'Very fresh steps, no?' the producer said to a distributor who had come to watch the shooting.

'Hmm,' the distributor said, picking some fried cashew nuts from the tray the production manager was holding in front of him.

Jumbo was sitting with the producer and the distributor on folding chairs in front of the boathouse. The three of them could have been brothers, they looked so similar dark, roly-poly, dressed in kurta pyjamas, thick gold chains strung around their necks. Jumbo fanned himself with his red check gamchha, bored and a little uncomfortable about not being in the driver's seat.

'Very nice costumes, Jumboji,' the producer said, and Jumbo brightened up at the compliment.

Mrignayani was dressed in an orange ghagra-choli that had been modified to look more sexy. The traditional ankle-length ghagra had been shortened to knee-length, while the choli had been reduced to a bikini top. The dupatta had been dispensed with altogether.

The next step that Rahul and Mrignayani had to do was completely ridiculous. They were made to sit face to face on a buffalo that was floating in the pond. Since morning, whatever attraction I might have felt for Rahul had been steadily evaporating into mid-air, but I couldn't help feeling a bit worried for him. Did buffaloes bite?

'Doodh jaisa pavitra mera pyar...' Mrignayani sang, thrusting out her bosom. The distributor looked at her appreciatively but Jumbo had a problem with the shot.

'Give Rahul something to do,' Jumbo told the choreographer. 'He's looking like an ass, just sitting there.'

'Umm... Right. Rahul, you splash water on her,' the choreographer instructed.

Rahul bent to his side and splashed water on Mrignayani, who shivered sensuously.

'That's yummy,' the choreographer yelled. 'More water.'

Rahul bent a little more, and lost his balance. He started to slide off, then grabbed Mrignayani's ghagra to steady himself. She threw her hands up, and almost in slow motion, both of them toppled into the water.

Mrignayani started shrieking her head off. The choreographer jumped into the pond and rescued her, while Rahul, who couldn't swim, had to hold on to the buffalo which kept slipping away.

Mrignayani threw a right royal tantrum, abusing everybody from Rahul Kapoor to the choreographer. Even Jumbo's attempts to soothe her failed – she pushed his arm off her shoulder and told him to shut up.

'Mehboob Khan is screwing her nowadays,' Manoj whispered in my ear. 'It's gone to her head.'

'Where's that asshole, Rahul Kapoor?' Mrignayani shouted. 'He can't get through two days without some accident happening to him. Bambai aaya hai hero banne, that bloody idiot!'

The idiot in question was sitting on the grass and sneezing, at the rate of twenty sneezes per minute. She obviously couldn't fight with him while he was in that condition, so she turned her ire towards Manoj, who managed to quieten her down by agreeing that all the abuse she heaped on him was completely justified.

'But it will take me at least two hours to get ready again,' Mrignayani sniffed finally. 'My hair-style is ruined, and of course I have to wear another costume.'

'What for?' said the choreographer, who turned out to be a truly innovative guy. 'We'll shoot the rest of the song with you two in wet clothes.'

So Rahul stood in waist-deep water, holding Mrignayani in his arms, and dipped her into the water at one, took her out at two, dipped her in at three and took her out at four. She did the one-two by thrusting out her bosom and pelvis in turn, all the while singing, 'Doodh jaisa pavitra mera pyar...'

'OK,' the choreographer shouted.

'Not OK.' The distributor stood up in his enthusiasm and slapped the producer on the shoulder. 'It's not "OK", saab. It's "Very Good". Mazaa aa gaya. I'm buying your Central India territory.'

'That got sold just yesterday night, after the trial screening. Take CP-Berar or Rajasthan territories. This film is going to set fire to the B centres,' the producer said.

'I'll buy both.'

The producer smiled slowly.

'All territories sold out,' he said. 'Party tonight!'

Manoj was a health hazard on the dance floor, so I stayed a good six feet away while dancing with him. He believed literally in 'letting go' – stomping violently on the floor and letting his arms swing around like he'd lost all motor control.

'Having fun?' he shouted over the music, moving closer to me.

'Yes, yes, very nice,' I shouted, taking two steps back and almost falling backwards. I hadn't realised that I was at the edge of the dance floor which the art direction guys had set up near the pond. Someone else hadn't been so lucky. The choreographer's assistant had fallen into the water, but by the way he was yodelling, he seemed quite happy there.

All of us had been working damn hard for the past two months and everybody was in a happy, boisterous mood. There were only three women in our regular unit – Mrignayani, her hairdresser and me – so the men were delighted that the dancers had stayed for the party. I wished that Manoj had shared their feelings about the dancers, but somehow, he'd decided that tonight was the night to woo me in style. His style – which consisted of demonstrating that he was a wild, energetic party animal who could satisfy whatever demands a woman might make on him.

Rahul narrowly missed being hit by Manoj when he tapped on his shoulder. Manoj looked irritated for a moment, then bowed graciously and put my hand in Rahul's.

I took my hand back, but told Rahul when Manoj left, 'Today, you're a real-life hero. You've rescued a damsel in distress.'

'Never fear, gentle maiden, I am always there for you,' he said, coming closer to me as the music changed to a soft, romantic number. 'All you have to do is call and...'

'Did you bribe the DJ to change the music?' I asked suspiciously.

'Who, me?' Rahul said, all injured innocence. 'First you put me on a pedestal and then you jerk it from under my feet. From hero to zero.'

'So what are you, actually? Hero or zero?'

'I'm just an ordinary human being, baba,' he said. 'You know, I was really scared today, during the shooting. Of the buffaloes.'

'You're scared? Of buffaloes?'

'You're not? That's great. You could have saved me then, if a buffalo had charged at me,' he said, smiling into my eyes.

I tried to look away, but somehow, it was very hard to. It didn't seem to matter that he was talking about the silliest things on planet Earth while gazing deep into my eyes. Oh well, what the hell, I was dancing with one of the most good-looking guys in town. Might as well look at him while I was at it.

I'd never noticed before that he'd got such long eyelashes. Not when I was writing continuity. Not even when I'd had that who-blinks-first match with him. His eyes were a warm, reddish shade of brown, like dark honey… 'Like chocolate cake fresh out of an oven' flashed into my head, and I laughed.

Rahul looked at me enquiringly but I shook my head. He gave me a mock-scowl, and I laughed even more. He touched my cheek with his fingers for a moment and then looked away. My heart was beating like an express train and no matter how many times I reminded myself that I'd spent half the day watching him prancing around with buffaloes, it refused to slow down.

Rahul tried to put his arm around my waist but I shook my head, moving back. 'I don't want to do a close dance,' I said.

'No close dancing. Just an old-fashioned waltz.'

He put his right hand on my waist and held my hand with his left hand, but kept a very respectable distance between us.

'I don't know how to waltz,' I said, sucking in my tummy and holding myself straight. His hand was on my waist – what if he felt a tyre of fat?

'It's very simple. I'll teach you. It's three beats to the bar, right?'

'Huh?'

'Listen to the beats. One, two, three. One, two, three…'

It was difficult to concentrate on the beats with him looking so intently into my eyes.

'Have you caught the rhythm?' he said.

I nodded.

'So, on the first beat, I put my left foot forward…'

We bumped into each other.

'No, no, you put your right foot backwards. Ya, right, like this. So that our actions are co-ordinated,' he explained.

We tried it again, and hurrah! it worked.

'Now, at two, you put your left foot behind...' His instructions stopped because the DJ suddenly changed to a fast, foot-stomping number.

'You didn't bribe him enough,' I giggled.

'Uh-oh. OK, I'll teach you to jive instead.'

So he did. Teach me to jive. I'd only seen jiving before in films and I couldn't believe that I was jiving myself. I was having a great time, not caring about Manoj who was dancing with one of the junior artistes, but casting funny looks at me. I whirled around before bending back into Rahul's arms. His feet tottered but he didn't lose his balance. Thankfully.

'Paro. You were supposed to turn around once more before you bent back like that,' he said.

'Sorry, sorry, sorry.'

We did it again, with him taking me through the steps one-by-one.

'At the first beat, we come close. Two, we go far. No, not so far. Ya, right. Three, we come close. Four, you... Hey, pay attention na, baba.'

'Ya, ya, just a minute,' I said. I could hear somebody shouting. That was Jumbo's voice, wasn't it? We gravitated towards the small crowd which was gathering near the boathouse.

'You'll do what I tell you,' Jumbo was shouting drunkenly at Mrignayani. 'You've been spreading your legs for everybody, don't give me moral science lessons now.'

'I don't have to sleep with the distributor-types any longer,' Mrignayani shouted back at him, equally drunk. 'I've signed two more films with Mehboob Khan, understand?'

'I understand, I understand everything. But you don't understand.' Jumbo swayed near her and put his hand on her shoulder. 'Just because Mehboob Khan is screwing you, you think you've become a big star. You don't want to...'

'Ya, ya, I don't want to sleep with pot-bellied old men like you. I've moved on in life, buddy. You'd better accept it.'

The music had stopped and everybody had gathered around, watching the fight. Jumbo, Mrignayani, and even the producer, seemed to be too drunk to care about the crowd, but the distributor looked like he was wishing that he were anywhere in the world except here.

'Arre, I've seen lots of two-day stars like her come and go,' the producer shouted. 'I know how easy it is to sign somebody and chuck them out.'

Mrignayani's confidence faltered for a moment, but she quickly got it back. 'That's why none of the girls in the industry fucks you,' she sneered at the producer. 'Everybody knows that you're not a man of your word.'

'Today, you're conveniently forgetting that I am the one who gave you a break. *I*,' Jumbo said, turning her so that she faced him. 'Just wait till Mehboob dumps you. You'll come crying back to me. I've seen hundreds of little whores like you. I'll show you...'

Rahul whispered to me that we should leave, but I just couldn't. I watched in horrified fascination as Mrignayani tried to wriggle out of Jumbo's grasp. She suddenly ducked.

He caught her dupatta and pulled her towards himself, but she flung it off and ran.

'Don't let that bitch get away,' the producer shouted.

'Arre, to hell with her, let her go.' Jumbo clutched Manoj's shoulder to stop him from going after her, then held on to him because he was tottering on his feet. 'What does she think – just because she's got big tits and a big ass, I'll roam around behind her all my life with my dick in my hand? Let her go – twenty more will come.'

'Why don't we get you a drink,' Manoj suggested, trying to lead him away.

'I'm not that kind of a guy. I can share,' Jumbo said angrily, staying put. 'If Mehboob wants to fuck her too, no problem, feel free. But I'm not going to take shit. I don't have to take shit from this kal ki chhokri. Who the fuck does she think she is?'

'There's another girl here, a dancer, if she'll do...' the producer held the distributor's hands apologetically.

The distributor nodded, looking awkwardly at the people who'd gathered around.

'Why just a dancer?' Jumbo said angrily. 'Somebody get that album of girls who've given their photos for casting. One phone call and any girl we want will come running.'

'Just give me half an hour,' the producer said, slapping the distributor on the back. 'I'll get you a proper actress, don't worry.'

'We should have done something,' I said to Rahul, shaking my head. 'How could all of us just stand around, just *watching* that whole tamasha?'

'What could we have done?' he said, concentrating on his driving.

'We could have done something, anything. I don't know.'

'It's their own private jhamela, baba. Forget about it.'

'How can you be so cool about it? Private jhamela! By the same logic, even Draupadi's vastraharan was the private jhamela of the Pandavs and Kauravs.'

Rahul slowed the jeep a little and turned to look at me. 'I understand your feelings, but you have to learn to take all this in your stride, Paro. You can't do anything about this scene, what's the point of taking tension over it? Mrignayani's been sleeping with Jumboji and the producer right from the beginning, you know that, don't you?'

'I never knew about the producer. But... but Jumbo's always so lover-like with Mrignayani, how can he try to make her sleep with that awful distributor? I just don't understand.'

'The distributor must have talked it over with the producer and Jumboji. The market's down, so whatever this distributor asks for, they'll give,' Rahul explained. 'Two months ago, even Mrignayani would have gone quietly, but now she feels that she doesn't belong to that category any more. Actually, I think Jumboji's been getting mad at the way she's throwing her weight around after she started sleeping with Mehboob Khan. This was the last straw. It's more a prestige issue for him than anything else.'

'Prestige?' I shook my head. 'These guys should be whipped in public, the way they treat women.'

'It's not such a black and white situation, Paro,' Rahul said.

'So, what is the situation, then?'

'When I came to the industry, I also used to think that actresses are exploited, but when I saw how these girls are ready to sleep with anybody who can help them get a role...'

'Oh, so it's the girls and not the men who are responsible for the casting couch, huh?' I crossed my arms and turned to look at him.

'See, it's all demand and supply. If there weren't any buyers, there wouldn't be any sellers. I'm a struggling actor myself. I know what it's like to go to producers' offices, begging for a role. I'm not blaming anybody, I don't want to be judgmental, but... some of these girls are so calculating – they'll only sleep with somebody who can give them a role. I know this director who fell in love with a struggling actress. They made such a cute couple, everybody thought that they're going to get married. But then his film flopped and she was out of his life before the film cans came back to the producer's office.'

I was so angry that I didn't say anything. Rahul stopped the jeep in front of my building. I opened the jeep door, then paused and looked back at him. 'What about those struggling actresses who're not ready to sleep around for roles? What happens to them?'

'See, it's getting a break that's crucial. Most film-makers are playing it safe nowadays and casting a Miss India or a well-known model if they want somebody new. It *is* damn tough for a girl who has no connections in the industry to get a break. Even sleeping with a producer or director doesn't guarantee a role. But it might help.'

'Don't these guys feel sick with themselves?' I said. 'I've come to Bombay from Amravati because I want to be an art director. Some poor girl comes here from Ludhiana because she wants to become an actress – how is it right to pressurise her to prostitute herself?'

'I see your point, Paro, but who's going to change things? There is an actors' union, but there is too much competition amongst the starlets for them to get together and decide not to submit to the casting couch. As for the men in power, what motivation do they have to change?'

'But don't they feel guilty?' I said angrily.

'They figure that they're not forcing anybody,' Rahul explained. 'They're only taking what is being offered, so what's wrong with that? And anyway, justifications aside, these guys are having a ball. Which man is not going to enjoy having these sexy young things throwing themselves at him? You say that these guys should feel guilty, but most of them feel so proud of their "conquests" – "X slept with me for that role," "Y stayed in my flat for three months when she first came to Bombay." You hear such stories, you don't even know whom to believe... Uh? Goodnight.'

I didn't bother to reply, just got out of his jeep and walked off.

'All men *are* bastards,' I said to myself, banging the gate shut behind me.

TEN

Jumbo wanted to chuck Mrignayani out and re-shoot the film. The producer wanted to forgive and forget, not because he was a very benevolent human being, but because of the cost of re-shooting. Finally, the two men reached a compromise. Mrignayani's role would be chopped drastically on the editing table and her importance in the film would be reduced by introducing another female character.

Munshiji was called to Jumbo's office and the situation explained to him. He took out his notebook and stared at it. While everybody stared at him.

Jumbo had made himself comfortable, taking off his kurta and lolling on the mattress that covered half the room, while all of us sat cross-legged in a circle around him. He was cleaning his ears with a matchstick and chomping on an apple. This was the first time I was seeing him eating something so healthy, so I guessed that he was feeling bad because of Mrignayani's comment about his pot belly.

The air-conditioner wasn't working, which made the dull orange room seem even more claustrophobic. The producer, who was sitting by my side, fanned himself with a copy of *Trade Guide*. I tried to avoid smelling his strong spicy perfume by taking in very shallow breaths of air. Manoj, who was sitting opposite me, could sense my discomfort and grinned at me. I refused to smile back. I didn't want to have anything to do with the seven men from our unit who were sitting in the room. Including Rahul. Especially Rahul. I couldn't believe that I'd been foolish enough to actually feel attracted to him.

'Let's give Mehboob Khan a sister,' Munshiji said.

'What can we do with her?' Jumbo wondered aloud, scratching his neck with his red check gamchha. 'She can get raped... or, no, she can fall in love with Rahul and try to kill Mrignayani or...'

'No, no,' the producer said shortly. 'Re-shooting Mehboob Khan's home scenes will cost fifty lakhs. Think some more, Munshiji.'

Munshiji went back to his pen and paper and started writing laboriously, nobody knew what.

'We will give Rahul a sister,' Munshiji announced finally.

'Wah, wah, Munshiji, you are a genius,' Jumbo declared and reached forward to clap him on the back, but Munshiji was sitting too far way and Jumbo fell on his side.

Jumbo covered up his embarrassment by pulling some purple heart-shaped cushions under himself. 'Let's have some beer to celebrate,' he said. 'Fuck the diet.'

So they opened some beer and passed it around while discussing whom they should cast.

'How about Rashmi?' the producer said. 'She's got big tits, that girl.'

'She's acting opposite me in *Jaan Ka Dushman*,' Rahul mumbled.

'Yes, you can't be a bhyanchod, can you?' Jumbo roared with laughter and of course, everybody else laughed along.

I got up abruptly. 'I have to go to Akbarally's in South Bombay to buy a duplicate blue umbrella for Mrignayani,' I said. 'The old one's got torn.'

'Mrignayani's out,' Jumbo declared. 'Mehboob Khan hasn't even bothered to call me about what happened. She's definitely out.'

'But the umbrella's been used in the first kiss sequence and we've shot only half of it, so if you want to shoot the rest…'

'OK, go,' Jumbo said dismissively, and went back to his beer.

I was putting on my sneakers in the outer room of Jumbo's office, when Rahul appeared, all smiles.

'I can drop…' he started saying.

'I don't want to talk to you.'

'Why? Hey, what did I do?'

'You're a slime-ball like everybody else here. I would quit tomorrow if I could,' I said, lacing up my sneakers tightly.

'But what did *I* do? Forget about making a pass at Mrignayani, I don't even feel attracted to her.'

'Like hell,' I said.

'I've never…'

'Rahul!' Jumbo's voice made him stop in mid-sentence.
'Go, go, your master is calling you,' I sneered.
'I'll be back in a minute,' he said, and hurried back into the inner room.

'So who do we cast as your sister, Rahulji, tell us, tell us.' Jumbo's voice followed me as I ran down the stairs. 'You have any recommendations? Feel free, feel free...'

The umbrella which I found at Akbarally's was the right size, but the shade was a bit different from the one we had. I wondered whether I should dump my perfectionism for once and just buy the damn thing. Why the fuck should I bother to put in my best for such a shitty production...
'Where were you?'
The umbrella fell from my hands.
'I was searching all over the place,' Rahul said. 'If you'd waited for just two minutes at Jumboji's office, we could've come together. It would even have saved... Hey, where are you going?'
He followed me down the steps of the department store. Ignoring him seemed too dramatic, so I turned around and told him coldly, 'I'm sorry, but I don't wish to speak to you about any non-work-related matter.'
'Why're you talking to me like that, baby...'
'Don't you dare baby me,' I hissed. 'I can't quit my job because of financial reasons, but I refuse to interact with anybody from that unit on a personal level.'
'OK, I respect your feelings, don't talk to Jumboji. Don't even talk to Manoj. But I had nothing do with what happened yesterday, and you like me.'

'Who, me? Like you?'

A fat woman with huge shopping bags in her hands had stopped by our side and was staring at us openly. I turned around and walked out of the door. Rahul stopped to say something to the doorman, and I slipped away to lose myself in the steady stream of office-goers. The road was more than forty feet wide, but there was hardly any space for vehicles on it. It was chock-a-block with people walking to the railway station.

One good thing about Bombay is that one can always lose oneself in a crowd. The good things about Bombay I could count on my fingers. I wondered now why I'd been so fascinated with Bombay while I was growing up. I'd felt like I was just waiting in the wings, biding my time in Amravati, and real life would begin in Bombay. The first few months after I'd come here had seemed like a dream come true. It didn't matter that I didn't have money to buy anything. I used to enjoy just walking around in all these big stores like Akbarally's and looking at the beautiful goods on display. Sipping coconut water on Marine Drive seemed to be the coolest activity on planet Earth. And of course, like a true-blue artist, I'd sit on the railings in front of Victoria Terminus, staring at the hordes of people streaming out and sketch them till the traffic policemen shooed me away. I'd made two hundred and seventy-six sketches in the three months I'd spent job-hunting. Every week I would send off a sketch to Ma with a note saying, 'I'm fine, don't worry about me.'

I knew that she worried anyway. I'd say to her, 'You've let me go to Bombay, now what's the point of sitting at home and worrying about me? I'm mature enough to take care of myself, baba.'

Fat bit of maturity I was displaying in Bombay. What would Ma say if she ever found out...

'You know something funny,' Rahul said, appearing by my side. 'I had to exchange a token for my bag from the doorman, and by the time I came out of the shop, you'd disappeared.'

'I did that deliberately,' I said, turning left at Flora Fountain on to the main road that led to the Gateway of India. I was trying to walk fast, but there were hundreds of people on the sidewalk, all marching towards the railway station. I was going against the flow, so it was like trying to drive the wrong way through a one-way street.

'Whatever for?' he said, all wide-eyed innocence.

'I told you, na – I don't want to talk to you.'

'Come on, jaan,' he said, walking on the road so that he could walk by my side. 'You don't have to...'

I saw the bus just behind him and my hand jerked out and pulled him back on the sidewalk.

'You're so dumb,' I shouted at him. 'That bus would've hit you right now.'

He smiled angelically. 'See. I knew it. I always knew it. You care for me.'

'I saved you 'coz otherwise Jumbo's shooting would have got screwed,' I said through clenched teeth, starting to walk.

'Oh-ho! So you care about Jumboji! "Dil ki baat kahin lab pe na aa jaaye..."' he started to sing.

I tried to push him off the sidewalk, but he leant backwards and then swung forward, rocking on his heels like a 'Hit Me' doll.

A group of men standing at a paan shop whistled. I shoved my hands into my pockets and started to walk.

'Hey, that was such fun, let's do it again,' Rahul grinned.

'Fuck off,' I said.

Never one to take a hint, Rahul fell into step with me.

'Look, if you follow me on the streets like this, people will mob you.'

'Nobody will recognise me,' he said. 'I look very different on screen.'

'Well, then, maybe I can tell them, I can shout it out, just so as to get rid of you.'

'I don't think that they'll mob me anyway,' he said sadly. 'I'm not a star yet, you see.'

I crossed the road in front of Jehangir Art Gallery and hailed a taxi.

'Churchgate,' I said.

'Won't go to Churchgate,' the driver said, looking straight ahead.

'OK,' I said, getting in. 'Take me wherever you will go.'

'Dhobi Talao,' he said.

I didn't have a clue where Dhobi Talao was.

'OK, fine, Dhobi Talao,' I said.

The driver turned the meter down. I watched in absolute exasperation as Rahul got into the taxi from the other side. The driver started the taxi.

'Stop!' I said angrily.

I got out as the driver started complaining, 'But you said Dhobi Talao...'

Let Rahul pay, I thought. If it hadn't been for him, I wouldn't even have got into the taxi in the first place. I strode ahead angrily through the crowd. I was so damn broke, the last thing I could afford was travelling by taxi.

I stopped at the crossing, wondering which way I should go.

'Turn left. Horniman Circle's a nice place in the evenings.'

Angrily, I turned right.

'Actually, even Marine Drive is not a bad idea. I'll walk behind you and sing songs.'

Out of the blue, he actually started singing, 'Ruk ja o jaanewali...' At the top of his voice.

I wanted to die with embarrassment as all the office crowd stared at us. I stopped short.

'Will you,' I said, through clenched teeth, 'stop singing if I talk to you?'

He nodded his head and clamped a hand on his mouth, cutting off the song in the middle of a word.

'I hate these bloody dramabaazis of yours,' I said. 'OK, fine, you wanted to talk, so let's talk.'

'Shall we,' he said, 'go to a restaurant and talk?'

'No. I prefer to talk this way. Walkie-talkie. Very nice.'

'Uh... OK,' he said, falling into step with me. 'Look, you were asking me how the casting couch works, and since I've been in the industry a little longer than you, I told you. That doesn't mean that *I* am like that.'

'You said, "Which man is not going to enjoy having these sexy young things throwing themselves at him?" You're a man, aren't you?'

'I am a man, yes, but I'd feel extremely insulted if a woman wanted to sleep with me just because she thought I could get her a role. On a scale from one to ten, my self-esteem would hit minus five,' he said, smiling.

What a conceited bastard! How could I have ever let myself feel attracted to this dumb asshole? Even worse, just because he was the only person in the unit I could talk to, how could I have been silly enough to start thinking he was my friend?

'What if you're old and fat and nobody wants to sleep with you otherwise? Then what?' I said.

'I'll have you by my side then – equally old and equally huggable. So I'll just disentangle myself from the struggler and say, "My dear young child…"'

'Don't drag me into it,' I snapped. 'I don't give a damn whether you yourself would use the casting couch or not. I just don't want to associate with anybody from that slimy unit.'

'But you're also working in this unit, same as me. How am I more responsible than you are for what Jumboji and the producer do?'

'I just took up a job here, because I was… having problems with my old job. I didn't choose to come all the way from my hometown to become a part of this industry.'

'So, what do you think, I shouldn't be an actor at all because the industry is a sleazy place?' Rahul said.

'What about what you said that day – the necessity to eat does not justify the prostitution of Art?' I said, then corrected myself. 'No, not you, that French film-maker of Saira's said that.'

'I'm not prostituting my art. I'm doing exactly what I've always wanted to do.'

'I don't know how anybody can *want* to work in Jumbo's films,' I said. '*Jumboji's* films. You're the only person who calls him Jumboji to his back.'

'I call him Jumboji because it's a habit. And to be honest, also because he does get to hear of it and he likes it.'

'Tell me, do you really respect him?'

'Professionally, yes. And that's all that I should be concerned with,' he said. 'He's a damn good director. He makes very entertaining films.'

'Entertaining films?' I shrugged and looked away. 'To each his own, I guess.'

Some books on photographic techniques displayed in a roadside bookstall caught my eye and I stopped to look at them. I didn't want to get into another discussion about Hindi films with Rahul, so I picked up *The Five C's of Cinematography*. It was beautifully illustrated, but much too expensive for me to buy, and I kept it back.

'Tell me,' Rahul said, as we started walking again, 'don't these kinds of things happen in advertising as well? The casting couch, I mean.'

'Maybe they do, but I never got to know of any specific instance. Maybe I was too naïve to see what was going on,' I said. 'What the hell, I suppose it happens everywhere. Maybe it even happens back home in Amravati, what do I know? Prostitution is not restricted to the Bombay film industry.'

'It's not exactly prostitution,' Rahul said.

'Isn't it?' I said.

He was quiet.

I shook my head and said, 'But you're right, I'm just as responsible as you are. OK, I'm not prostituting myself, and of course I'm not a client, but is it justifiable to work as a cook in a whorehouse?'

'I understand how you feel, but my point of view is that as long as I'm clean, it's OK. What other people do is their business,' he said.

'How would I know what all you've been up to? I mean, being a part of the industry...'

'But Paro, I really have never used the casting couch, I'll swear to it. Cross my heart and hope to die, strike me dead if I tell a lie,' he said seriously.

'I'd better get away before that thunderbolt strikes,' I said, smiling wryly. 'Anyway, I'm sure that you don't have the clout right now to give a break to a girl. And if the girls are as calculating as you say, none of them would sleep with you even if you wanted to.'

'That's true, but it's a matter of principle. I have to prove it to you that I'm not that kind of person...'

'How does it matter to me what kind of person you are?' I said, and tried to change the subject. 'Have you been to the Jehangir Art Gallery lately? They have a...'

'I don't want to talk to you about painting right now,' he said crossly.

'Great,' I smiled. 'Don't talk to me then.'

'You can't just fling that accusation at me and simply walk away.'

'OK, baba, talk.'

'It's a funny thing to say, but I'm a nice guy. I really… Hey, what happened?' he said, noticing that I was no longer walking by his side.

'No, nothing,' I said. I'd stopped because I'd realised that walking so fast wasn't doing any harm to anybody except me. Rahul wasn't even out of breath.

'I'm thirsty,' I said. 'Let's have some tea.'

We sat at a corner table in an Irani café and ordered tea and cheese sandwiches.

'I love these old Irani cafés,' I said. 'They're so much more aesthetically pleasing than all these fast food joints. Round marble-topped tables and round wooden chairs…'

'Don't change the subject,' he said.

'What's the point?' I sighed. 'How does it make a difference what you really feel? I mean, to me.'

'Are you sure it doesn't make a difference?' he said, looking into my eyes. My heart gave a little leap. Stupid. Stupid. Stupid.

'It's not a big deal either way.' I shrugged.

He looked down at the checked tablecloth and said, 'I don't know about you, but it makes a major difference to me what you think of me.'

I shrugged again.

'I've never made a secret of how much I like you,' he said seriously.

'Yes, you haven't,' I smiled.

'Look, I don't know how to say this without your misunderstanding, but, like... trust me.'

I burst out laughing.

'I mean it,' he said sheepishly. Then, 'You know, you're turning it into a joke and treating trust like it's a dirty word, but it's not.'

'Talking of jokes, I heard a new one recently,' I said. 'Do you know why the Sardarji stopped sleeping with his wife?'

He refused to ask why.

'Because somebody told him that it's not good to sleep with married women.'

I knew it was a really poor joke, but he didn't even crack a smile.

'This is not a laughing matter,' he said angrily. 'I'm serious.'

'OK, serious, serious,' I said, trying to hide my smile.

He looked at me, exasperated, and then changed his track.

'Tell me,' he said, putting the tips of his fingers together like a professor. 'How do you define the word trust?'

'I don't know. I'm not a walking-talking dictionary.'

'Patience is an extremely important virtue,' he said to himself.

'Your tea's getting cold,' I said.

He ignored it.

'What I mean is, what does the word "trust" mean to you, personally?'

I made a face. 'It's a bit like faith, I guess. You believe that God exists and that He's good even though there's no concrete proof.' I took a sip of tea and another thought came to me. 'That's why it doesn't make sense trusting people. Because people aren't as good as God. Except mothers, maybe.'

Not all mothers, my brain nudged me. My baby must have trusted me... Come on, Paro, it was just one inch long. What would it know of trust? It wasn't even a real baby, I told myself.

Rahul leaned back in his chair and said slowly, 'When I was doing theatre in Delhi, we used to play trust games. You've heard of trust games?'

I shook my head.

'They are games that a group of people play together. You start with falling backwards with your eyes closed. You know that there's a person behind you who will catch you properly before you hit the floor. It's very hard to do in the beginning. Your eyes instinctively fly open as you feel yourself falling backwards, your arms go out to save yourself – but slowly you learn to trust your partner and let yourself fall without the least bit of fear. In fact, by the end of it we were falling backwards from a height of six feet into the hands of a group.'

'That sounds impressive. But why do all this in the first place?'

'See, theatre involves a lot of teamwork, and trust games help you to come closer as a group. You learn to trust others and be trustworthy in turn. You learn to be alert when you are doing the catching, because you know what it's like to be in the shoes of the person who's depending on you. But more than anything else, it teaches you to let go of the fear within you. It teaches you that it's safe to trust.'

'Sounds nice,' I said, crossing my arms.

'Oh, it's beautiful, it makes you feel so free,' he said, leaning forward.

'But I'm sure that some people must be falling and hurting themselves, na?'

'They're very rare, but ya, accidents do happen sometimes,' he admitted and frowned as he took a sip of his by-now stone cold tea. 'But there are so many people who have accidents while, say, riding bicycles. I'm not saying that there isn't any risk, but that one trusts taking the risk into account. Because if we didn't take any risks, we would be absolutely paralysed. Tell me one thing you can do without any risk whatsoever.'

'I can drink this glass of water,' I said, and proceeded to drink it.

'How do you know absolutely hundred percent for sure that it's not poisoned? The waiter might be a nut case, maybe he doesn't like your face and...' Rahul made a gesture of emptying a packet into my glass of water while looking around surreptitiously, stirred it with a spoon and served it to me with a toothy smile.

'Umm... I could lie in my bed all day.'

'How do you know that there's not going to be an earthquake?' he said, getting irritated but trying not to show it. 'Or that the roof won't decide to cave in? Huh?'

'It doesn't seem very probable,' I said, looking away from him. Why did he have to look so attractive when he was angry?

'Right,' he said. 'The probability. That's the crux of the issue. In other words, the risk...'

'I remember how bored I used to get in school doing all those "Calculate the Probability" sums,' I said and lit a cigarette. He leant forward, took the cigarette from my hand and ground it out in the ashtray as I watched, astounded.

'Another defence manoeuvre?' he said.

'Rahul, you're getting agitated. I mean, this is just a discussion...'

'Why the hell shouldn't I get agitated? It's the question of our life together. We're going to be so bloody happy, you're not going to believe it. You'll get down on your knees someday and thank me for having had this stupid discussion with you and convinced you.'

'Like a Hindi film heroine,' I smiled.

He refused to smile back.

'You keep on putting me down whenever I say anything emotional. You think only Hindi films have melodramatic dialogues? People do speak melodramatically in real life too,' he said. 'All the emotions we depict on screen are taken from real life.'

'"I need you,"' I hammered. '"I need you like my bones need calcium and vitamin D."'

Rahul smiled a bit reluctantly, but he did smile.

'Well, but I'm sure somebody or the other has used that line even in normal life,' he argued.

'Inspired by Hindi films,' I grinned.

'I shouldn't be telling you this,' he said, 'but when I was in school, my best friend had to be admitted to hospital because of fainting spells. He'd been writing letters in blood to woo this girl he was in love with. Long letters.'

'Did she also fall in love with him, finally?' I asked.

'No,' Rahul said, sadly.

'Tell me something,' I said, 'do you have a pattern of falling for hard-to-get women?'

He covered his head with his hands and moaned.

I looked around from the corner of my eyes. 'Don't,' I hissed. 'People will stare at us.'

'Let them,' he said, looking at me from between his fingers. 'Let them know what you're doing to me.'

I pulled his hands off his face. He grinned at me. I felt like pushing back the mop of hair falling on his forehead, but I told myself that this look was designed to make women want to do just that. Didn't his make-up man style his hair into careless disarray before every single take?

'Tell me, if I were hard-to-get, would you be interested in me?' he said.

'Why don't you try? Seriously.'

'Aha, I sense a calculating mind at work here.'

'Maybe you ignore me for two-three weeks and *I'll* be buying you flowers. Worth trying out, na?'

'Hmm,' he said contemplatively. 'Hmm.'

'Hmm,' I said, my hand covering my smile.

'Was your ex-boyfriend hard-to-get?' Rahul asked. 'How did you fall for him?'

'Oh, with him it was love at first sight. He walked through the door and I went plop!' I said. I was trying to be flippant, but actually, it wasn't very far from the truth. The first time we met, Karan had given me a friendly smile and said hi. I'd forgotten to say hi in turn and cursed myself for the ten days it took him to speak to me again. I'd desperately search for excuses to discuss something with him and then be so tongue-tied when he talked to me, I was sure he must've… Cut. N.G. Let it be, na, Paro. What's the point in thinking about it any more?

'What about him, how did he fall for you?' Rahul said.

'He fell for me when, at least he said he did, but then maybe he was just… Oh, I don't know,' I said. 'I don't know what to believe any more.'

'He is so much a part of your life even now,' he said gently. 'Why don't you… tell me about him.'

'What's there to tell?' I said. 'His name is Karan, he's a cameraman, I met him when I was working for Mr Bose. We went around for… what? Four months? He was playing around behind my back, but I never knew about it, it's not like I broke up with him because of that or anything, he was the one who dumped me and, and… what else? That's it.'

'I'm sorry,' he said softly.

'I'm not sorry,' I said defensively.

'I understand what you're going through. I've been through a heartbreak myself. The past is dead, let it go. If you keep on referring to it…'

'Oh, I'm sorry, I didn't know that I'm boring you with all my references to my past,' I said, furious. I hadn't volunteered to tell him my life story. Who the fuck was he to pass judgement on it?

'I'm not bored. I just wanted to help you look at things in the right perspective, so that you can heal…'

'I've healed alright now,' I said shortly. 'I don't cry over Karan any more.'

He swirled the remains of the tea in his cup and looked at me. 'There's a quote by Amrita Pritam that I really like. "Peace is not just the absence of violence, peace is when the flowers bloom."'

'You know why you keep on quoting people? It's because you're too dumb to have any original ideas of your own. It's good that you're an actor – speaking lines other people have written for you.'

'What do you get out of putting me down so much?' he said angrily.

'I'm sorry. I've never been so rude to anybody before, but... but why do you make me talk so rudely to you, Rahul, why can't you take a hint and lay off?' I said, fed up. 'Do you think I enjoy it, being so rude to a person? I have to keep on putting you down more and more – it just doesn't seem to have any effect. Don't you have any self-respect? Why do you take it? I snub you so badly. Why do you take it?'

He leaned back in his chair and looked at me through a glass. 'Maybe I've fallen in love with you.'

'Really?' I snapped. 'That's interesting.'

He didn't say anything, and I started feeling like a heel. There. I'd done it again. From where had I learnt to be so rude? What if the poor guy really did mean it? I took a deep breath and said, 'I'm sorry about what I said to you.'

'It's OK. I understand.'

'*What* do you understand, baba? In fact, I don't know why you even started liking me in the first place.'

'You looked very lost, very hurt. I wanted to be your knight in shining armour, I guess.'

'Bhagwan bachaye mujhe,' I muttered. 'Anyway, look, things would never work out between the two of us. I'm too old for you.'

'What too old? You're only two years older than me.'

'Mentally, I'm at least five years older.'

'You think that being bitter is being mature,' he countered.

'Come on, Rahul, you're so, so... kiddish most of the time.'

'I just act kiddish because it makes you smile,' he said suavely. 'You have a lovely smile.'

I shook my head, but I did smile.

'Thank you. I suppose you even fell into the pond that day to make me smile, hmm?'

'Oh, that!' He gave me a mock-scowl. 'I was drowning and all of you were laughing. Dancing on a buffalo looks so ridiculous that it seems easy, but it's not, let me tell you,' he said, trying to look dignified.

'The sacrifices one makes for the cause of Cinema,' I murmured, and called for the bill.

'Sacrifices, right, absolutely,' he grinned. 'I even got a catch in my arm when I fell off the buffalo.'

'Major sacrifice,' I said. 'Heroic.'

'Or maybe it was when I picked up Mrignayani. She's heavy, you know. All that dipping her into the water and taking her out,' he complained, rotating his wrist.

'Nobody who sees the film is going to have the remotest idea about how much of an effort it took you to do that step,' I said mock-sympathetically.

'Nobody,' he grinned.

I offered to pay, and he let me, which was nice for my ego, but bad for my purse, since the bill had come to seventy-two rupees. Perhaps there would come a day when I would look back nostalgically at my 'being-broke-in-Bombay' days. I hoped that day would come soon.

ELEVEN

I couldn't hide my shock when I saw Jumbo and Mrignayani arriving together in his red Mercedes at the dance rehearsal hall. But Manoj wasn't even surprised.

'The lovers' tiff is over,' he said, smirking.

Jumbo, with his arm around Mrignayani's waist, was cracking jokes and she was giggling happily. I looked at them and then looked away, trying not to think about the night of the party and what had happened later. Jumbo and the producer had even gone as far as casting a starlet to play Rahul's sister, a song had been composed for the new-found sister to sing at a carnival which had been written into the script, and our set was being done up for this carnival. Today was supposed to have been the starlet's first day of work with us, rehearsing the dance at the dance rehearsal hall. I gritted my teeth, telling myself that somebody much wiser than me had said that all's well that ends well. Who the fuck was I to mind?

Things seemed even better than well with the pair now. Jumbo was going all out to make it up to her. He patted her every two minutes, made her eat silver-covered paan with his own hands, even decided in the middle of the dance rehearsal that the dance should be a solo performance – Mrignayani looked sexier dancing alone than with Rahul.

'How can you chuck me out of the song, just like that?' Rahul protested.

'Are *you* telling me what I can and can't do?' Jumbo glowered at Rahul, asserting that just because he had taken Mrignayani back, it didn't mean that he was a pushover. 'Don't try to throw your weight around, you don't have any.'

I'd seen Rahul in the most miserable of situations, including trying to hold on to a buffalo in a pond, but somehow, I'd never felt sorry for him before. Maybe because he was trying so hard to cover up his disappointment by laughing and joking with Manoj and the choreographer.

'Roll sound,' Jumbo called out.

Rahul refused to watch Mrignayani as the music started and she went through the steps all alone. The dance rehearsal hall was just a big, bare room with mirrors on all the walls, and he had to pretend to be busy with his mobile to avoid looking at anyone.

'Main hoon mirchi…' Mrignayani lip-synched, pressing a huge plastic green chilli into her bosom.

'It's such an inane dance,' I said to him when he came to return the kneepads to me.

'Yes, but now I'll have only two songs picturised on me in the entire film,' he explained. 'Mehboob has four songs. It's not even a decent second lead any more.'

'What'll you do now?' I asked.

'I'll go to town and see *Sholay*. It's running in a theatre there.'

I'd meant to ask him what he'd be doing about his role in the film, but I said encouragingly, 'That's nice. It'll be fun watching it on the big screen.'

'Why don't you come and see the film with me?' he said.

'I would have loved to, but I'll be busy with the rehearsal all day,' I said kindly.

'How about Saturday night, then?'

'I think we'll be shooting the song by Saturday.'

'Friday, then?'

'Uh no, we'll be doing up the set on Friday,' I said, wondering how I'd ever got myself into this discussion.

'This evening after the rehearsal would have been great, but I have to go for a costume fitting,' Rahul said, consulting his Filofax.

'Ya, tonight would have been great,' I said.

'I'll cancel my costume fitting,' he said quickly.

I laughed out loud.

This definitely was not Rahul's lucky day. The theatre was House Full. The police arrested a black-marketwala just as Rahul approached him. And to top it all, it started to rain. That too, not a light drizzle, but a straightforward downpour, Bombay-style, like God had opened a tap in the sky.

We were drenched to the skin by the time we managed to find shelter in a roadside tea stall. Rahul couldn't stop apologising.

'I've been asking you out so many times and the first time you agree...'

'Second time,' I reminded him, wringing the water out of my dupatta.

'OK, second time. And we end up in a place like this,' he said, looking around at the little shanty that consisted of a blue plastic sheet held up by two bamboo poles and the compound wall by the footpath. It was just six feet by eight feet, but it seemed to be doing good business with about half a dozen people drinking tea and eating hot bhajiya. A man dressed in a torn vest and a knee-length lungi was frying the bhajiya on a kerosene stove near the wall.

A grinning boy made space for us on a rickety bench, and without being asked for, two glasses of cutting chai were placed in our hands.

'Think of all the money you've saved,' I said, ordering kanda bhajiya.

'I'm broke, but not so broke.'

'You're a star, how can you be broke?' I asked curiously, warming my hands on the glass of tea.

'The big money will come only after I'm established,' he said. 'Till then, anybody who's casting me is doing me a favour. I have to agree to whatever money they offer.'

'Oh, like that,' I said, remembering the way he'd taken being chucked out of the song picturisation. 'I was thinking, maybe, Jumbo will put the buffalo song back, now that he's made up with Mrignayani.'

'But they've changed the script and recorded this new song,' Rahul said.

'They can always change the script again,' I said.

'They can always do anything,' he grinned.

'Right,' I said and dug into the steaming hot kanda bhajiya that the smiling boy placed in front of us. I immediately ordered another plate of bhajiya because, as I explained to Rahul, 'It should be ready by the time we finish this one.'

'Tu hero hai, na?' the boy said to Rahul, digging his hands into the pockets of his half-pants.

Rahul nodded, thrilled to bits.

'Maine *Maut Ke Sikandar* dekha hai,' he informed us proudly and marched away.

'Congrats,' I said to Rahul, smiling.

'No, nothing like that,' he said shyly.

The boy took a big bamboo and poked it into the blue plastic overhead, making the water that had collected on top of the plastic spill out. The breeze blew it on two men who were sitting nearby and they shouted at the boy. But he just ignored them, stylishly twirling the bamboo over his head.

A remix song that combined the Spice Girls' 'If you wanna be my lover' with the 1950's Hindi film song, 'Saiyyan dil mein aana re', played on the rickety old radio near the man who was frying bhajiya. The sound was full of static, but it didn't matter, and I happily tapped my foot to the rhythm.

'Why don't you eat?' I said. 'You hardly eat anything at all.'

'I'm eating, I'm eating,' Rahul said, popping a bhajiya into his mouth. 'Don't you have to watch your weight?'

'Watch weight? Bah! Who for?' I said, biting into a fried green chilli. '*You* should. Watch your weight. Otherwise, your female fans will be very disappointed. Do you actually have any? Female fans, I mean.'

'Ya, a few, I guess,' he said, looking a bit sheepish. Then, 'I once got one hundred and seventy-two letters. After my interview was published in a Hindi magazine. They gave my address at the end of the article.'

'Huh? One seventy-two?' I stopped eating to look at him. 'Wow, man, that's a lot. Did you write back?'

'Not personal letters, no – that's not supposed to be a good idea. I just sent postcard-sized photographs with my autograph. Anyway, that was about one and a half years ago – just after *Maut Ke Sikandar* was released. Now I'm lucky if there are two letters a week. It all depends on the releases. Another film of mine, *Paapi*, is being released in five weeks. Let's see what happens then,' he said, brightening up.

'But what if it flops?' I said tactlessly. 'What will you do if, say, all your films flop? I mean, of course I hope they don't, but…'

'I hope so, too,' he said, knocking on the wooden bench. He shifted a bit to avoid the rain that had changed direction and was blowing right into the tea stall. 'I have thought about that. Television, maybe, though I hate soaps.'

'Can't you do any other work?'

'Ever heard of the acting bug?' he grinned. 'It doesn't let go easy. No, but let's suppose, hypothetically – just hypothetically, mind you – suppose I don't even get work in TV, what then?'

I was starting to feel bad that I'd ever asked.

'I could go back to Delhi, complete my graduation... but no, I won't give my father the satisfaction of being right.'

'Then... what will you do?'

'I almost went back home once,' he said suddenly. 'I was acting in *Maut Ke Sikandar*. Second day of the shoot. The director wanted a very real Bombay feel to the film – crowds and local trains and slums and – have you seen the film?'

I shook my head, feeling a little guilty.

'Anyway, the film opens with me getting stabbed in broad daylight on Marine Drive. The director decided to shoot the scene with a hidden camera, to get authentic reactions from the crowd. So here I am, walking down Marine Drive, and four men with choppers get out of a car, attack me and jump back into their car and zoom off. The craziest thing was that it's such a busy road, but not one person came to help me. I lay on the road bleeding to death as far as anybody knew.... Fifteen minutes I lay there, I know because the assistant director counted. The cars would slow down, then speed up again. Nobody cared, nobody wanted to get involved. Even the people travelling in buses – such utter indifference, it was scary.'

Rahul finished his tea in one gulp and shook his head, staring at the empty glass. 'I told the director – "I'm leaving Bombay. You can take your fame and money and do whatever you like. I don't want any of it." I was just seventeen then, so... But I didn't leave finally.'

I almost felt like holding his hand, but of course I didn't.

'You got killed in the first scene of the film?' I said, for want of anything else to say.

'No, no,' he said, starting to smile. It was nice to see his dimples coming back. 'I get stabbed, and everybody thinks that I'm dead. Same with the other three guys – Kuldeep gets drowned, Jayesh Khanna is shot and Salim Sheikh is... I don't remember... Yes, he falls from a big cliff. But we all survive. That's why we're called *Maut Ke Sikandar* – the conquerors of Death.'

'Wow,' I said, shaking my head and laughing.

'I know. I think my director probably took inspiration from Jumboji. Hey, I know what I'll do if I flop completely.'

'What?'

'I'll join Jumboji as an assistant director.'

'Or you could even become a dress-man. They get paid better than assistant directors,' I said. 'You know Bihari, na – he's the chief dress-man in our unit. He ran away from home to become a villain in Hindi films. He never got a break. He tried his hand at some real-life villainy, joined a gang in the slum where he was living. His first job was to evict a family from a hut. He was getting along fine, throwing out pots and pans from the hut – when the people in the area got together and beat him up so badly, so badly, he decided he was better off becoming a dress-man.'

'"Madam, your costume for the scene – yellow hot pants and orange blouse, madam,"' Rahul said, rolling his eyes like Take Two.

'And white shoes,' I added.

'What about you?' he said, 'What will you do after Jumboji's film is over?'

In about five months time, Jumbo's film would be over. I felt incredibly much so cheerful when I thought of that prospect.

'Well, ultimately, I want to design sets, so I have to work towards that. I mean, not for Hindi films, I don't think I can handle the set-up. So, after the film is over, I guess I'll look for a job in advertising. Or maybe I'll just go home for a while and eat ghar ka khaana.'

'And get fat,' he grinned.

'So?' I showed him my tongue and ordered a plate of aloo bhajiya.

'Jeena isi ka naam hai...' I sang along with the car radio happily.

'Uhu-uhu,' he cleared his throat and turned down the radio.

'Hmm?' I turned to look at him.

'You might be thinking,' he said seriously. 'That just because I've gone out with you means that I'll let you kiss me. But I'm not.'

I opened my mouth to protest, then realised that he was throwing my lines back at me, and shut up sheepishly. He ruffled my hair and kissed me. On the cheek.

Choosing a dress to wear took me twenty seconds most mornings. Today was not most mornings. I'd already spent ten minutes deciding what to wear and ten more trying to find a black dupatta to go with a maroon kurta and black chudidar. I had a maroon dupatta and chudidar which went with my maroon kurta, but I didn't want to wear that because

Rahul had told me just yesterday that maroon was his favourite colour, and he'd think that I'd dressed up for him.

I finally found a cream dupatta and chudidar to go with the kurta. They went well together, in fact they made me look so pretty that I felt like putting on lipstick. A bit of kajal followed, and the silver jhumkas cried out to be worn and... I looked in the mirror and I knew that if Rahul saw me like this, he'd definitely think that I'd fallen for him.

I ended up going to work wearing a white shirt and blue jeans and red eyes because I'd had to use soap to wash the kajal out of my eyes. As it turned out, I needn't have bothered. Rahul hadn't come to the rehearsal hall that day.

As a matter of fact, nobody had come to the rehearsal hall when I got there. I'd rushed in, fifteen minute late – to be brought up short by the lock on the door. It feels so nice when one is late to find that other people are even more late.

I was sitting on the steps and smoking a beedi I'd bummed off a spot boy when Manoj drove up in a bottle green Opel Astra.

'What happened to the local?' I asked him, laughing. 'Common man, remember?'

'I did it, I did it for three whole months. I have an idea now, that's enough.'

Mrignayani was in her element as she and the choreographer worked on perfecting yet another variation of the pelvic thrust.

'Tilt it up more and shiver it a little,' the choreographer shouted over the music. 'Yeah, yummy.'

I wanted to get out of there, not because I was embarrassed (I was past that), but because I badly needed a cigarette. I'd almost managed to slip out of the hall by the side door, when Jumbo called out to me.

'Paro,' he said almost apologetically, 'can you go to the set and check out how work is coming along on the stage?'

'Yes, sure,' I said, relieved to be getting out of there.

'Don't worry, after you've checked up, you can come back here,' Jumbo said kindly, patting my arm. 'This is where all the action is.'

Mmm. It was the best smell in the whole wide world. Paint and turpentine. I breathed in deep, right down to my stomach. I was just supposed to be supervising the art direction guys, but when they'd gone off for lunch, I hadn't been able to resist picking up a brush. The stage backdrop was so big, I figured that it didn't hurt any if I painted a bit. And I was happy like a child, doing what I loved more than anything else – painting.

I added two broad strokes of red, then a squiggle of blue, smudged gently. My hair came loose as I bent down to dip my brush in the turpentine.

'Ofoh!' I said, without turning around. 'Where did you come from?'

Rahul tied my hair into a knot and stuck the pin back in.

'I wanted to check how work on the stage was coming along,' he said unconvincingly. Then, 'I thought you might be feeling lonely – all alone on this big set in the middle of nowhere.'

'I was enjoying my solitude,' I said, but smiled at him from the corner of my eyes.

I added a yellow line next to the blue and smudged it with my fingers.

'What do you think of it?' I said, stepping back.

'It looks, well, kind of... like a cat.'

I'd been painting a depiction of Shiva and Shakti.

'You could have said something worse, I suppose. Though I can't think of much,' I said.

'Oh, it's not so bad, I like cats,' he said.

'I prefer dogs.'

'I know what you mean. Dogs are loving, trusting creatures. You know what the trouble with cats is? If a cat sits on a hot stove once, she won't sit on a hot stove again. But the problem is, she won't sit on a cold stove, either.'

'Tom Sawyer said that,' I said accusingly.

'I wasn't trying to steal his quote. And it's Mark Twain, not Tom Sawyer.'

'Ya, ya, same thing. Anyway, why do we have to talk, and analyse, and discuss so much?' I asked, adding some blue to the design. 'Can't you think of anything better to do?'

He took the paintbrush out of my hand, kept it in the mug of turpentine, and kissed me soundly on the lips.

'That wasn't what I meant,' I said, feeling shy but trying not to show it. I rubbed the paint-mark on my cheek. He kissed the mark. I tried not to look at him, but when I did, I couldn't help smiling. He kissed my lips again, softly.

I wouldn't have minded if that kiss had gone on forever, but the sound of footsteps made us disentangle quickly.

'I was thinking, Madam is all alone, it's not good for me to be taking rest,' the painter, who'd come back early from his lunch, said sweetly.

'That was really very nice of you,' Rahul said, hamming a hearty smile and clapping him on the back.

I was feeling so shy, that I started acting brash. Rahul was happy, stretching, singing, 'helping' me with the painting (he couldn't paint for nuts), kissing me quickly when the art direction guy's back was turned.

Rahul's jeep wouldn't start. As usual. But neither of us minded in the least. We walked halfway to the Film City gate, holding hands, before we saw a bus. It appeared on the horizon, and as it inched towards us, it started to rain.

The wizened old conductor stared at us disapprovingly when we clambered in, dripping water and giggling like mad. We sat as far from him as we could and held hands.

I had never seen Bombay looking so beautiful before. Not just the lush green of Film City, even the crowded roads looked charming. Maybe it was because of the rain.

'Close your eyes,' Rahul told me.

'But what about the conductor?' I said, shocked.

'Smell the rain, dumbo.'

I closed my eyes and I could smell the smell-scape – Rahul's after-shave, the gajras at the stoplight, bhuttas being roasted, and below it all, the musky scent of rain meeting parched earth.

'It's been discovered that the typical "first rain" scent is caused by the spores of some bacteria being released into the air,' I informed him, but my eyes were laughing.

He gave me a mock-scowl and put an arm around me, not drawing away even when the conductor passed by, coughing disapprovingly.

'In a Hindi film, this would have been a song,' I giggled.

And he turned to me and started singing, 'Pyar hua ikraar hua hai...'

I told myself that it is was the most predictable song to sing under the circumstances, but my heart melted and flowed down, right out of my toes. 'Parvatitai,' I told myself, 'if you don't watch out, you're going to fall in love with this guy.'

'I'm feeling so happy and so scared because I'm feeling so happy,' I whispered into the phone. It was two o'clock in the night, definitely not the most decent of times to be chatting on the phone, but Saira came back late from work so this was the only time I could catch her.

'What are you getting so hyper about, sweetheart?' Saira said soothingly.

'He's a Hindi film *actor* for God's sake!' I groaned.

'He's dishy,' she commented.

'Karan was dishy too. I thought that I'd learnt my lesson from that whole episode. But no. Here I go again. Aa bael mujhe maar.'

'Maybe it's real love,' she said doubtfully.

'I don't know about real love, but it definitely is real lust,' I laughed.

'That's great,' she said. 'What's stopping you, then?'

I hesitated. Somehow, I didn't want to tell Saira.

'What's the matter, sweetheart?' she said.

'I feel very attracted to Rahul, but even now, my body seems to belong to Karan. In a funny kind of way, I feel like I'm being unfaithful to Karan by thinking of getting involved with Rahul. Maybe unfaithful not to him, he never bothered to be faithful to me even when we were together. Maybe, unfaithful to my love for him...'

'That's all the more reason why you should get involved with Rahul. It'll help you break your attachment to Karan.'

'I don't know,' I said, shivering as the windows opened with a bang and the wind blew a spray of drizzle on me. I closed the windows quickly, stealing a look at the landlady's bedroom door. I was breaking one of her rules – traipsing around the living room in a nighty – and if she found out, there'd be hell to pay.

'Why don't you just have an affair with Rahul?' Saira suggested. 'Just have some fun, that's all.'

'With Karan...'

'See, with Karan, you were emotionally involved, that's why it hurt you so much that he just wanted to fuck you. Because you wanted different things from the relationship, right?'

'Uh-huh.'

'Look, that's what *I* feel. If you go and talk to Kavita, she'll tell you that all men are bastards, you're better off by yourself. You know what a bloody pessimist she is,' she said.

Saira had recently gone and made up with her Whacko. Even I hadn't been too happy about it. But my disapproval was nothing compared to Kavita's. She'd laid an egg when Saira had forgiven Whacko for slapping her because he'd been tripping on speed and hadn't realised what he was doing.

'Kavita's so bloody self-righteous! I don't know how – what do they say – how she always knows what's good for everybody else,' Saira complained. 'I don't even know what's good for me.'

'The most irritating thing is that she's usually right,' I said.

'Ya, I know,' Saira said moodily. 'Maybe you should ask her, then…'

'I'll ask her later, but right now, I'm asking you,' I said. 'What do *you* think?'

'I would advise you to get on with your life,' Saira said. 'You used to be so bubbly when you first came to Bombay. But after everything happened… Means, you've become so serious and bitter nowadays. Nothing like a bit of romance to cheer you up, get things into perspective. But that's just my opinion. You have to make your own decision based on what you want.'

'But how am I going to find out what I want unless I talk to you?'

'Ya, you're right,' Saira laughed.

'Actually I don't think that I'm in love with Rahul either,' I said, going on, stronger now. 'I mean, of course I'm very attracted to him, and he's really fun to be with, that's all.'

'That's cool, then,' Saira said. 'Enjoy.'

'Ya, like MTV. Enjoy.'

TWELVE

Why do men have to be so contrary? Now that I'd decided to have an affair with Rahul, he seemed to have stopped chasing me. He'd said hi in the morning when he walked into the set, and then he'd disappeared. He wasn't required for the shoot till afternoon, but I'd expected him to hang around like he usually did, chatting with the choreographer and, of course, flirting with me. Was he playing…

'Paro!' Manoj shouted. 'You look so bloody lost, I'm going to file a missing person report about you. Get Mrignayani ready. Fast.'

'Sorry, sorry,' I said, then I remembered. 'But I've already sent her costume to her.'

'Well, do something else then. Fast.'

I ran to help a bikini-clad dancer who was struggling to adjust the ten-foot wide wings she was carrying on her back. Manoj was very worried because the pre-monsoon rains had started earlier than usual. We had to finish shooting on the set before the monsoon destroyed it.

I tightened the waist belt and shoulder straps to which the dancer's wings were attached. She gave me a quick smile and ran towards the stage, her pink and purple wings billowing behind her.

Our set had turned into a riot of colour with carnival floats and giant masks and more than a hundred dancers dressed up as Koli fisherwomen, cheerleaders, belly dancers, witches and pirates. Co-ordinating all these elements would have been a difficult task anyway, but the pressure of doing everything fast was making everything go haywire. The camera was supposed to crane down as a dozen butterfly dancers trooped on to the stage. It was a simple shot in principle, but problems kept on cropping up. Three of the dancers' wings got entangled with each other and when Manoj tried to free them, the wings got torn. He started shouting at the dress designer who'd made the wings, but Jojo, the choreographer, soothed him and said that the shot could be taken with just eight dancers.

The next time, the dancers managed to get to their positions on time, but the crane operator, who was a new chap, moved the crane too slowly. And then – it started to rain.

A light near me went off with a flurry of blue sparks and the light-boys switched off all the lights on the set. The camera attendants covered the camera with a black cloth and carried it into a verandah, shooing away the dancers who were in their way. Everybody scattered, running for shelter. Everybody, that is, except the producer, who stood his ground and started giving ma-bahen ki gaalis to Jumbo.

Jumbo called out softly for his spot boy who was carrying his umbrella, but he was nowhere to be seen. Jumbo reluctantly stepped out of the verandah into the pouring rain and confronted the producer.

'How come everything that goes wrong is my fault?' Jumbo shouted back. 'Even the rain is my fault, huh?'

'You bastard, you said the shoot will be over by the end of May. Today is the...'

'What am *I* supposed to do? Mehboob Khan gave us twenty shifts, but he's come for only twelve. You get him here for...'

I slipped away to look for Rahul. Borrowing an umbrella from Take Two, I searched everywhere – the Costume Room, the verandah in front of Mehboob Khan's house, even the production manager's office – and found him where I least expected him to be. His own changing room. He was dozing in a chair, his feet propped up on the dressing table.

I whisked my dupatta lightly over his face. He smiled without opening his eyes.

'Which perfume do you wear?' he asked.

'No perfume-sherfume. I can't afford it,' I said, leaning back on his dressing table. 'That's sandalwood-scented talc.'

'Smells yummy,' Rahul said, smiling lazily at me.

'Are you avoiding me?' I said suddenly.

'Why should I be avoiding you?' he said.

'I don't know. Maybe you're angry at me for some reason. Or maybe you think that I'm going to assume too much and start doing a needy, clingy act, or whatever.'

'It's "angry with", not "angry at",' he said, smiling. 'And no, I'm not avoiding you.'

'What? Oh, like that,' I said. 'I suddenly realised – when you're angry with a person, you're "with" him in a way.'

'Hmm,' he said.

I sniffed. I thought it was quite an insightful observation, but if he didn't want to appreciate it – pearls before swine.

'I'm just feeling very bugged that they're shooting the song without me,' he said. 'It's got nothing to do with you.'

'Oh, OK. I'm sorry about jumping to conclusions,' I said, but I wasn't sure whether I should buy this explanation. Rahul's behaviour seemed suspiciously similar to one of Saira's 'he disappeared the morning after and never called up again' stories.

'I wish I could tell them to get lost...' he said. 'But no, Jumboji's right, I shouldn't try to throw my weight around, I don't have any.'

'I understand what you're going through, but I, like... I wanted to know – what happened yesterday, was it just a one-off or do you want something more long-term?'

Saira and Kavita would probably kill me later for asking such a direct, put-him-in-a-corner question, but what the hell. I definitely didn't care enough about Rahul to play games with him.

He *was* looking a little panicky. 'Long-term, as in, marriage and all? See, struggling actors earn peanuts and I...'

'Don't be silly. I'm not talking about marriage, for God's sake. You don't have to feel scared, I'm not even remotely interested in marrying you.'

'What would you like?' he said cautiously.

'Actually, I was also thinking, why do we have to get so serious about this whole thing? Let's have just an affair, na.'

'What do you mean by "just an affair"?' he said.

'"Just an affair" means, like, we don't get too senti about each other, and there's no need for other people to know about it, and stuff like that.'

'Suits me fine,' he said, looking a little relieved.

Oh. So that's all that he'd wanted too. I made myself shrug away my irritation. Saira had gone around with so many guys and enjoyed it in quite a light-hearted way. Why couldn't I?

Rahul claimed to be broke, but he lived in a 1BHK on Yari Road. A one-bedroom hall kitchen flat. The living room was furnished quite well, with a comfortable sofa, wall-to-wall bamboo chatai and twenty-five-inch television. There was no colour scheme as such – bright yellow, light blue, olive green and lavender cushions rested comfortably on the reddish-brown sofa. The bookshelf was dark pink and the curtains were made of light green cheesecloth. It had obviously not been designed in any way, but the total effect was of a happy, relaxed place.

I wandered over to the bookshelf. There was an odd medley of books on the top shelf – Shakespeare's soliloquies, *How to Become a He-Man in 90 Days*, Milan Kundera's *The Unbearable Lightness of Being*, James Hadley Chase's *Miss Shumway Waves a Wand* and more than a dozen dog-eared low-calorie cookbooks.

The kitchen looked like he actually did use those cookbooks. It wasn't just the fancy-looking gadgets which were kept neatly on black metal shelves – there were more than thirty different varieties of pulses in clear plastic jars. As proof that they hadn't been bought for their decorative value, three batches of sprouts of various pulses were being prepared in a four-compartment plastic sprout-maker.

The bedroom was as messy as the kitchen was neat, but Rahul cleaned it up in one minute flat. The heap of clothes on the largish single bed was stuffed into the cupboard. All the towels and clothes on the floor were tossed into the laundry bag. A fresh blue bedspread was laid on the bed and voila! The room was presentable.

'You can see the sea from here,' he said, drawing the curtains and showing me the view from the window. 'See, from between these two buildings. I call it my piece of the sea. It looks really lovely when it rains.'

'Oh wow!' I said, but I wasn't looking at the sea, I was just taking in the number of skin care products on his dressing table. 'You use all this... yourself?'

'What? Oh... Ya.'

I was still looking at him, surprised, so he explained. 'Hey, man, I'm an actor, I have to take care of the way I look.'

'Uh-huh,' I said, trying not to laugh. Somehow, it seemed terribly unmanly to be using so many beauty products.

'If I don't look good, none of these guys are going to take me in their films.'

'But you've got *Fair and Lovely* here!'

'See, as far as I go, I like the way I look when I'm tanned. But I play the hero, and the hero has to encapsulate people's aspirations. What can I do if Indians have a colonial hangover?'

It was obvious that he was using this intellectual jargon to cover up his embarrassment, so I smothered my laughter.

'All this is for the cause of Cinema, hmm?' I said.

'You know, Paro, when you're *there* under those lights, and the camera starts to roll and the director shouts, "Action" – it's a mind-blowing high. It's better than anything else in the whole wide world.' He looked at me, his eyes shining. 'Except, of course, holding you in my arms.'

'Hah! That was just an afterthought.'

He laughed and I felt a twinge of jealousy.

'Someday you'll be a big star and you'll have all these pretty young things throwing themselves at you,' I said.

'There's something I've always wondered about,' he said seriously. 'It's never happened to me, but I keep on hearing about all these fans throwing themselves at stars. What exactly do they do?'

'Catch!' I laughed and charged into him. I should've known better. He toppled over. Thankfully, we fell on the bed and neither of us got hurt. Taking full advantage of the opportunity, he started to kiss me. I wriggled away, feeling shy, and feigned interest in the music cassettes that were stacked on a bedside table.

'Oh, I hate acid rock.' I looked at him, pained. Because of my room-mate, I'd listened to enough acid rock and heavy metal to last me a lifetime. Make that several lifetimes.

'OK, we'll listen to R.D. Burman. You like R.D., right? See, I know you, I know what you like, even before you say it...' he said, kissing my neck. 'You have such beautiful skin, so soft...'

He was undoing the buttons on my blouse and kissing my neck. I unhooked the clasp on my bra because he just couldn't seem to open it, but when he kissed my breasts, I started to shiver so badly that I had to draw back.

'Just a minute, just a minute, please,' I said, my voice also shaking like an idiot's. Even my hands were shaking as I tried to hold my blouse closed.

'What happened?' he said, reluctantly letting me move away.

'No, nothing,' I said, leaning over the edge of the bed to locate my purse. I bumped into his chin as I was coming up.

'Sorry, sorry,' I said, moving away from him so that I was sitting on the corner of the bed. I sneaked a look at him. He was lying on his side, leaning on an elbow, looking very confused.

'I was shaking like I'd got malaria,' I said, laughing with embarrassment as I lit my cigarette.

'That's OK, na?' he said.

'It was, like, a bit too intense.' I buttoned my blouse, and putting my hands under it, hooked up my bra.

'Scared?' he said.

When I didn't reply, he took my hand in his and kissed my wrist. 'Don't worry, I won't hurt you.'

I took my hand back from him and made a face. 'Oh come on, I'm not scared of the pain. I'm not a virgin or something.'

There was a short pause as I puffed away at my cigarette.

'I wasn't talking about that,' he said.

I closed my eyes for a moment, then burst out, 'Why do I have to be so dumb? So, so, dumb. All the time, with my knee-jerk reactions. How do you take it? Why do you take it?'

He drew me close and cradled me in his arms.

'Do you know,' he said after a while, 'how you should make love to a porcupine?'

I couldn't see his dimples, but I could feel them with my cheek as I waited.

'Very carefully,' he said, bursting into laughter.

I hit him on the head with a pillow and then threw it at him as he rolled to the other side of the bed.

I looked away, then looked back at him and smiled.

'Why don't you have an ashtray?' I gave him a mock-scowl, as I ground out my cigarette in the packet.

'I don't smoke. I'm a good boy, I am.'

'A good boy, hmm? Don't tell me *you're* a virgin,' I said.

'Well, not that good a boy.'

'How did you... like, lose your virginity?' I asked, hiding my smile with my hand.

He hid his face behind a pillow and then hugged it, giving me a mock-scowl. 'Why do you want to know?'

'Oh, come on, just like that,' I said.

He hemmed and hawed and finally said, 'Auntyji... There was uh... this lady who was our neighbour. She seduced me when I was fifteen.'

'This Auntyji,' I asked. 'How old was she?'

'In her thirties, I guess.'

'Was she married?'

'Ya.'

He seemed none too keen to volunteer information, but I was feeling too curious to be tactful.

'Did she, like, have any kids?' I asked.

'Two boys. Twins, studying in primary school.'

'Did you always... call her Auntyji?'

He burst out laughing.

'You want to know everything, don't you? Ya, I did, even in bed.'

'Well, what happened, then?' I said. 'How long did you guys stay together?'

'I'd just got to the point where I'd started satisfying her, you know what I mean, and then my elder brother found out. I got the thrashing of my life and he threatened to tell Mama, so, well, that was the end of that.'

'Oh. And afterwards?'

'They shifted to Lajpat Nagar after a year or so,' Rahul said. 'I always suspected that she had something on with the chowkidaar, but I didn't ever find out for sure.'

'No, no, I didn't mean your Auntyji, I meant with you, what happened to your love life after that?'

'Oh, like that. There was this really pretty girl who was working with me in our theatre group in Delhi. That was real love. But she got a scholarship to study in the US, so she left. And then, in Bombay, there were a couple of girls, nothing serious. And then, ya, that's it,' he concluded.

'I was thinking...' I said.

'Yes?'

'About... uh, like, about AIDS.' After my abortion, Saira had made me read a detailed article about sexually transmitted diseases. 'And Hepatitis B and C and... and...'

'And A?'

'I don't know if that's transmitted like that. Anyway,' I said, my cheeks burning. 'No exchange of bodily fluids.'

I didn't know if that was the right way to put it. The article hadn't been that specific.

'OK,' he said, looking at me from behind the pillow.

'And anyway, anyway, I don't want to... to go all the way with you.'

'Why?'

'Because it's too... uh, too...' My vocabulary had gone for a toss. I wished I had a cigarette in my hand. 'It's too... intimate.'

He looked at me without saying anything.

'But we can do "Everything But",' I offered quickly. 'It's lower-risk as well.'

'What is "Everything But"?' he asked. I didn't want to look at him so I was looking at the idol of baby Krishna on his bedside table. Very nicely done, in white marble.

'"Everything But" means...' God, why had I ever gotten into this? 'Means doing everything except "it".'

'Hmm,' he said.

Last night, when I'd decided that I would be able to handle our 'just an affair' much better if I didn't have sex with him, I'd never thought that discussing it would be so awkward. I told myself that I should be feeling proud of myself for being so assertive and direct, but all I felt was horribly embarrassed. I'd never even talked to Karan about these matters. I started scraping the chipped nail polish off my toenails, then realised that Rahul was watching me, and quickly pulled my skirt over my feet.

'I know of one very low-risk activity we can indulge in,' he said. I looked up. He rolled near me, drew me into his arms and gave me a big, warm bear hug.

THIRTEEN

'You fill up my senses like a night in the forest...' I hummed under my breath and hugged the song to myself. Rahul had sung it to me in bed this morning. Last night was the first time I'd stayed at his place and all the colours looked brighter today. The salwar kameez I'd worn instead of my regulation jeans was loose-fitting, but the material was soft and it made me feel... Mmm, sexy. I even felt looser, nicer from inside. Maybe what they said was true, after all – sex is good for health.

Vaise, we weren't really doing *it* as such. We'd stuck to 'Everything But' in spite of his protestations.

'Hey, man, you're taking the fun out of sex, making it so clinical and so... so regimented.'

I'd given him one look.

'It's OK, it's OK,' he'd said quickly. Then, starting to grin (that bloody grin, it was irrepressible), 'It's very hard to take *all* the fun out of sex, no matter what you do. I guess we'll get by.'

When I caught sight of myself in the Costume Room mirror, there was a wide smile on my face as well. I realised that I was grinning like an idiot and tried to stop, but it kept on popping up like a jack-in-the-box. I gave a 'cheer up' smile to Jumbo who was sadly examining the paint flaking off the exterior of the church on our set. I smiled brightly at Mehboob Khan when I was noting down his costume continuity. I even gave a warm smile to Shweta before going to bed. Actually, it wasn't very hard to give Shweta a smile that night because, for a major change, she wasn't playing any music. Her tape recorder had conked out.

It was such a pleasure, just letting myself drift off to sleep. Expecting night-crickets in Bombay was a bit too much, but the soft whirring of the fan and the commentary of a football match somewhere in the background formed an ambience highly conducive to sleep. Sleeping with my head under the pillow was definitely not necessary tonight.

In times past, I had often daydreamed of doing some violence to her music system. I had been barely able to hide my glee when she told me that the motor had got burnt and she wouldn't be able to repair it for a while. God had answered my prayers.

It wasn't as if I were an Aurangzeb – I did like music, especially the John Denver numbers that Rahul had played last night. I was missing him a little. A little? Well, a little goes a long way, as the ad says. Rahul was dubbing tonight. Not for Jumbo's film, that still had three more weeks of shooting left. Rahul was looking forward eagerly to the release of this other film. I wondered what would happen to us and our 'just an affair' if he became a star, then dismissed the thought from my mind. What was the point of worrying about far-fetched things?

Jumbo had asked Manoj and me to assist him with the editing, so I didn't have to worry about finding a job for at least four months more. Maybe I would go back to advertising after that. It would be such a relief to be out of the Hindi film set-up. And advertising paid much better money than feature films, so I wouldn't be so broke. I didn't mind continuing to stay with Shweta if she didn't play music... The light was on since Shweta liked to read in bed, but sleeping with the light on was no big deal. I coughed. About the cigarettes, well, I'd stopped minding Shweta's smoking after I'd started smoking myself, though I did mind the way stale smoke hung around our room. Ya, perhaps I could invest in a second-hand exhaust fan from Chor Bazaar if I got a good job... I coughed again. What the hell? That wasn't cigarette smoke.

I turned around and shrieked. The mattress between Shweta and me was on fire.

I ran into the bathroom. The bucket was full of my wet clothes. Filling it would've taken too much time, so I just picked it up, ran into the room and emptied it on the mattress.

The fire spat angrily, a big cloud of smoke rose in the air and then, everything was quiet.

'Shweta!' I shrieked. I couldn't believe it. She was still asleep.

She woke up slowly and looked at me groggily, barely able to keep her eyes open. I was panting, holding the bucket in my trembling hands.

'Why...' she swallowed hard. 'Why have you kept your wet clothes on the bed?'

'These girls... my mattress... my bed...' Some words escaped in short gasps from the landlady's red face. The rest were lost within.

'The mattress cost six thousand two hundred rupees,' the landlord said sternly, his eyes glued firmly to the cleavage that was revealed by Shweta's low-cut nighty.

The estate agent tut-tutted as he inspected the mattress. A part of my head filed away how the burn marks looked. Never knew when one would have to create that effect. The fire had formed a crater of sorts – scorch marks in a diameter of about twelve inches, burns in a gently sloping radius of four inches, going down to a depth of about three inches. The fact that all this and more was soaking wet did not make things look any better.

'It's a real foam mattress,' the landlord said. 'Cost six thousand two hundred rupees.'

'It's probably possible to repair it,' I put in. At first, all I'd felt was murderous anger at Shweta and her bloody cigarettes. But since then, the landlady had been informed and she'd told us to get out of her house, and the estate agent who'd got us the place had been hauled out of his bed in the middle of the night to arbitrate.

'We... We'll pay for the repairs,' I offered.

'It's one solid piece of foam,' the landlord said. 'Cost six...'

'The bed,' the landlady shrieked, suddenly getting her voice back. 'It's burnt. See, see.'

It wasn't really *burnt*. It just had soot marks on it. I bent down and tried to rub them off.

'She's trying to hide it, look, look,' the landlady shrieked at her husband. 'I'd told you that we shouldn't keep girls. And this estate agent you found, look at what faltu girls he brought here – coming back at all times in the night, wearing all sorts of indecent clothes, burning my furniture with cigarettes... I don't care if we don't get the extra money. I won't have my house burning down around me. No. Just no,' she said, shaking her head emphatically.

The landlady's kid picked up a couple of lipstick-stained cigarette stubs from the floor and showed them to the estate agent who tut-tutted, shaking his head. Shweta took a dupatta that was lying on the chair near her and draped it around herself. The landlord looked away reluctantly.

'I want them out of my house tomorrow,' the landlady said to the estate agent.

'Look, please...' I said.

'You just get out of my house.'

'What do you mean? Where will we go?' I cried out.

'I'm not saying, "Get out tonight." I can't kick out a woman in the middle of the night,' she said.

'But you can kick her out any day, huh?' My voice was shaking. I couldn't believe this. I turned to my agent. 'She can't make us leave without notice, can she? One month's notice. It's written in my contract.'

'Yes, Madam, but there's one more clause also, no, after that? That clause no. 5 – "party in the second place,"' the estate agent read out slowly from the contract, '"will vacate premises immediately, upon the discretion of party in the first place, if conditions 2.b or 3.c are violated." 2.b is... "The furniture and..."'

'You should be on our side,' I shouted at him. 'You've taken two month's brent... brent... I mean rent as brokerage from both of us.'

'We also gave him one month's rent,' the landlady shouted at me.

I was so angry, I wanted to cry. First of all, I'd almost been burnt to death because of Shweta's stupidity and now, on top of that, I was being kicked out of my place. I turned to Shweta, who'd been quiet throughout all this.

'Please,' Shweta said pleadingly to the landlord, letting her dupatta slip down a bit.

'Out,' the landlady shrieked, stomping out of our room. 'Out.'

'Dil bhi khaali, ghar bhi hai khaali, isme rahegi koi kismatwali,' Rahul sang to me. I said no, but I smiled.

That was the only time I smiled that day. I'd woken up with a start in the morning to see our landlady standing by our bed staring malevolently at us. 'Six o'clock deadline,' she said, and left.

Shweta packed up and moved out soon after. I managed to pat her on the shoulder and say, 'Hota hai. Everybody does silly things sometimes.'

I called up Manoj and told him that I couldn't come for work that day since I had to find a place to stay. When he started grumbling, I told him angrily that if it just wasn't possible to spare me right now, I could pile on at his home till the shoot got over. I was sure that his parents would understand. They were film people, after all... He quickly gave me leave.

'It's June, na, that's why no paying guest room available now. Schools, colleges, everything starts in June. Too much demand,' the agent told me. It was less than nine months since we had renewed our contracts, so he was obliged to find us a similar place without charging any brokerage for it. 'Why don't you go and stay with some friend or relatives for a while?' he suggested.

The landlady peeked in for the fourth time in the day as I sat on the floor, trying to pack my things. I didn't know how I had managed to collect so much stuff. I had come to Bombay with just two suitcases. These two suitcases had been filled long ago. I was starting on my seventh big polythene bag now.

And I still didn't know where I was going to go. Kavita stayed in a hostel and Saira's landlady had a strict 'No Overnight Visitors' rule. Rahul seemed to be the only option, but I didn't want to pile on. Both of us had agreed that our relationship was going to be a light-hearted one. I'd stayed at his place for the night just once. To move in two days later, bag and baggage, was too much. I racked my brains. Who else was there? Who could I stay with?

I called up Sharmishtha but she hemmed and hawed so much, I said, 'It's OK,' and hung up quickly, cringing inside.

I got up and walked slowly to the landlady's bedroom where she was combing her daughter's hair.

'Hello, please...' I found it hard to plead, but there didn't seem to be much choice.

'Six o'clock,' she said, without looking up.

I almost burst into tears when I saw the drawer that Rahul had emptied out for me in his bedroom cupboard.

'Hey, hey, don't cry,' he said, alarmed. He tried to take me in his arms but I moved back.

'I'm not crying,' I said, biting my cheeks from inside. 'I wanted to tell you that I'm really grateful for today. And that this doesn't have to mean anything, I mean it doesn't have to mean that we're living together or anything.'

'Ya, ya, of course, no sweat.'

He stood around for a while, then scratched his head and said, 'I'll make some more space for you.'

'No, I just... don't be so... You don't have to be so nice to me.'

'But you will need some more space,' he said, looking at my two suitcases and seven big polythene bags.

'I really don't know where so much stuff came from,' I said helplessly. 'When I first came to Bombay I had only two suitcases. You don't know how terrible it was – packing – with the landlady, that bloody bitch, hovering around. She kept on peeping in and saying, "Six o'clock deadline," "Six o'clock deadline."'

'You should just have bought a big carton from the kiranawala and put all the things in that instead of so many plastic bags,' he said.

'What? Ya, I guess so.'

'I'll get you some tea,' he offered.

He was looking so awkward standing in the middle of the bedroom, that I made myself snap out of my mood.

'I don't need more space,' I said, getting up. 'I've kept all the stuff I need immediately in the small suitcase. The rest of the bags I'll keep... Where shall I keep them?'

'Under the bed?' he said.

'Will do. And you go and make some tea now.' I gave him a kiss on the cheek and a gentle push in the direction of the kitchen.

All the clothes from my small suitcase managed to fit into the drawer. I kept my underclothes hidden under a dupatta, then blushed when I realised that he'd see them anyway.

I suddenly remembered that I hadn't left any forwarding address or phone numbers at my landlady's. What if Karan called? What if, in an impossible Hindi-filmi way, he wanted to make up with me and couldn't get in touch? Maybe it was because of Rahul, but the thought didn't wrench my heart so much any more. Of course, he had my email address, not that I actually wanted him to... Omigod, what if Ma called? She hardly ever did – we didn't have a phone at home and she thought STD calls were an unnecessary extravagance.

But what if there were an emergency? I decided to call up my uncle in Amravati and let him know Rahul's number, just in case. I could... yes, I could tell him that I was staying at Saira's place and this was her landlord's phone number.

What if Ma ever found out what I was up to? How would she react if someone told her that her darling youngest daughter was having 'just an affair' with a Hindi film actor, and even living with him? She wouldn't believe it. She just wouldn't. Last week she'd sent me a letter saying, 'Has Karan told his parents about you? I'll go and talk to them…'

Rahul peeped into the room and blew me a flying kiss. I caught it in my hand and solemnly kept it in my pocket. He started walking towards me but the sound of milk flowing over the rim of a hot vessel made him run back into the kitchen.

I was staying here for just a while, I told myself. Just a while, till the estate agent found us a place.

A week passed, two, but the agent had shown Shweta and me nothing except a much smaller room that cost, crazily, two and a half times as much. I suspected that the reason for the shortage of paying guest rooms might've been that he wasn't going to get any brokerage for the deal. But he stoutly denied it when I accused him. 'You don't have trust in me, Madam? I am honest broker. Next week, I find you room,' he told me. 'A-class room, A-class landlord. Don't worry, madam. Next week.'

I'd stayed overnight at Rahul's place once, but living with him was totally different. Sleeping in his arms on a single bed felt very nice and cosy, but in the beginning, I found it very difficult to actually fall asleep. More than feeling uncomfortable, I kept on worrying about whether *he* was feeling comfortable.

For the first few days, I was on my best behaviour – making the bed as soon as I got up, clearing up the dishes and making sure that my clothes never strayed anywhere out of the drawer except on the clothes line, and of course, on me. Generally, trying to be as small and inconspicuous as possible, to take up as little space as I could. But Rahul seemed so comfortable with my presence and happy to have me around, I started to relax and enjoy myself.

I'd forgotten how nice it was staying in a proper flat after all those months cooped up in a single room. With Shweta, at that. But much more than all the practical stuff, what I really enjoyed about staying with him was that we were always cuddling. Sometimes, well, maybe more than sometimes, it developed into more than just innocent cuddling. But Rahul seemed to enjoy holding me and hugging me just for its own sake as well, not like Karan who used to get so turned on if I touched him that...

'Stop thinking of him.' Rahul bit my nose playfully.

'Ooh, ooh. What?'

'No entry for ex-boyfriends in my house,' he said, trying to look casual, but I could tell that he was pissed off.

'I wasn't thinking of my ex,' I said.

'Oh yeah?' he said, crossing his arms.

'Sorry, sorry,' I said, uncrossing his arms and putting them around myself. I couldn't keep my curiosity back and had to ask, 'How did you know that I was thinking about...' I sneezed. 'About Karan?'

'I know because I am this sensitive, liberated metrosexual man who is so perceptive that...' He put on a pompous tone, then laughed. 'Actually, it's because you get this pained, martyred expression on your face, like a goat being taken for slaughter.'

He made a strange face and bleated painfully. I burst out laughing and hit him with a cushion.

'Why can't you take inspiration from Meena Kumari, why do you have to take inspiration from goats? Did you know that Meena Kumari...' He stopped in mid-sentence as the title music of *Saddi Dharti Sadde Log* came on. For some unknown reason, he *had* to watch *Saddi Dharti Sadde Log*, a program about farming, at 12:30 every night. It came on some obscure Punjabi channel that I'd never even heard of. He watched it with rapt concentration, no disturbances were allowed. I didn't really mind, just snuggled into his arms, burrowing my face into his kurta, eyes closed, feeling the gentle rise and fall of his chest.

'You know, they say that you find out strange things about people when you start living with them. Like, who'd have thought that suave, debonair Rahul Kapoor *has* to watch *Saddi Dharti Sadde Log* every single night? How long have you been doing it?'

'About a year,' he said sheepishly, like he were revealing a guilty secret.

I bent down to ruffle his hair, then straightened up carefully. Rahul had picked me up and put me on top of the fridge, because he said that I interfered too much with the cooking. Have I talked about his cooking yet? He was, simply, the best cook in the whole world, even better than my mother. Vaise, he preferred to eat out, but I loved staying at home. After all that mandatory eating out, plus, of course, milk powder with cornflakes and water, ghar ka khaana was like manna from heaven.

'Maybe I'll become a farmer some day,' he said thoughtfully.

'Do your people own land, back home?'

'My grandfather did, but there were a lot of fights over the property, so my father just said that he didn't want his share. One can always buy some, I guess,' he said, adding the onions to the tadka. 'If you're a farmer's wife, nobody'll blame you for being fat.'

'I'm not fat,' I cried out indignantly. 'I'm just a bit plump, that's all.'

'More of you to love,' he said, adding the tomatoes. He turned around, made me bend and kissed me – till the tomatoes got cooked.

FOURTEEN

'You're getting a piloerection,' I said to Rahul as I adjusted the collar of his costume.

'What?' he said, shocked.

'You know, all these hair on your arms and all, standing up on their ends, that's called a piloerection.' I walked away, laughing softly, as he tried to keep a straight face.

I shivered and when I looked down at my arms, I smiled. I'd got a piloerection of my own. I wished that I were wearing something more substantial than a cotton T-shirt. The time was around midnight and it had been drizzling lightly. Not that the spirits of our unit members were dampened in any way. It was the last day of the shoot, and booze had been flowing like water since sundown. Jumbo had handed over control to the choreographer and was moving around the set like a genial host, backslapping everybody from the spot boys to Mehboob Khan.

I was glad that we had managed to complete our shooting on the set somehow or the other. The rain had reduced it to tatters, so we were doing this song picturisation at night, with what Manoj called 'Expressionistic Lighting'. Which just meant lots of shadows and silhouettes, with lights placed behind the church and the houses near the chowk where we were shooting. It looked stylized and saved us the expense of renovating the set.

I smiled gratefully at a spot boy who gave me a glass of hot tea, and leaned on the railing, watching Rahul dancing frenetically with two scantily-clad dancers. The girls had such wow figures, it was hard not to feel jealous. I sucked in my tummy and it looked flat. But drinking tea that way was tough, and after five minutes, I let it puff back to normal. Depressed, I stared at the girl in red who Rahul was dancing with. Her waist was at least five inches smaller than mine. And her breasts were perfectly formed hemispheres that peeked out provocatively from her low-cut choli. Probably assisted by a push-up bra, I thought unkindly. Or breast enlargement surgery.

But I doubted that Rahul was thinking of all these things as she arched over him, her breasts just inches away from his nose. He picked her up and she put her legs around his waist and leaned back, her long hair sweeping the ground. Throughout this whole manoeuvre, they kept on shaking and smiling for all they were worth.

'Shake, shake, harder, harder,' the choreographer shouted encouragingly.

'One minute break, please,' Rahul said, putting the girl on her feet. His personal spot rushed to him and gave him a cup of tea. The personal spot boy was a new addition – Rahul's latest release, *Paapi*, was doing well in the Delhi-Uttar Pradesh territory, and the producers who visited the sets needed to be impressed. Rahul was still broke, of course, but he said that he was investing in his image.

'My teeth are going to fall out,' he said, coming and standing by my side. '"Shake, shake, harder, harder."'

'You look like you're enjoying yourself,' I said, trying not to sound jealous.

'You *have* to look like you're enjoying yourself, otherwise…'

'What is this, just tea? Hah!' Jumbo swayed towards us, holding a glass of whisky and soda in one hand and a bottle of beer in the other. 'Have, have. Have whatever you want.'

'Thank you so much, Jumboji, but…' Rahul tried to keep his balance as Jumbo put an arm around him and slumped. 'But I've got to dance, na? Tough dance, shake, shake, shake.'

'No problem, it'll give you some masti. If you're happy, audience will also be happy.' Jumbo forced the beer on Rahul, who took a few sips, then held the bottle loosely in his hand.

'Good boy.' Jumbo patted his back. 'Good dancer. Very flexible.'

'I'm nothing compared to those girls,' Rahul said, pointing to the dancers who were trying out some new steps. 'Especially that one in red. She's terrific.'

'You want her? No problem,' Jumbo said, clapping his back. 'Anybody you want, no problem. Tonight, party night. Free for everybody. Manoj told you about air-conditioned van, no?'

'No, no, thank you, Jumboji,' Rahul said hastily, giving me a look. 'I'm feeling much fresher now, Jumboji. Thanks for the beer.'

Jumbo gave him a hug and pushed him forward. 'Go out there and show the bastards what you can do. Jor lagake haiya!'

I wanted to ask Rahul what Jumbo had meant about the air-conditioned van, but he got so busy with his 'shake, shake' rehearsal that I couldn't. The van was parked near the temple under the banyan tree, far from where we were shooting. There was a cluster of men standing around it, and I was wondering whether I should go near and check it out, when I saw Manoj and Kapil standing in the market lane, sharing a beer.

'Hey, Manoj, what's this funda about the air-conditioned van?' I said.

'Nothing for you, baby,' he said, grinning widely and trying to slip an arm around me.

'But what *is* happening?' I said, trying to stay out of his reach.

'Why? You're also interested? Hey, Kapil, she also wants to have a go.'

Manoj and Kapil dissolved into laughter. I waited for them to finish, a polite smile stretching my lips.

'Arre, three dancers are there. Anybody wants – go and do jhig-jhig-jhig. Open house. Party night. Hey, this Take Two also went. How was it, Take Two?'

Take Two started denying it, blushing. I walked off.

I was trying to tell myself that it didn't matter, that I'd always known about Mrignayani and Jumbo and all, but I couldn't help the nausea that was threatening to come up. I went and sat in a corner inside the verandah of Mehboob Khan's house. The music reached me loud and clear, but at least I couldn't be seen from outside because of the bougainvillaea surrounding the verandah.

I heard Manoj calling out my name a couple of times, but I ignored him. To hell with the costumes. I hoped that there was some mistake with the continuity, it would serve them right. No, that was too little, I hoped that the lab chewed up all their negatives...

'Hey, where have you been?' Rahul said, peeping into the verandah. 'Jumboji's been calling you...'

'Fuck off.'

'Huh?'

'Leave me alone,' I snapped.

'But, hullo? What happened?' he said, coming to sit by my side.

'Do you know what's happening in the air-conditioned van?' I said angrily.

'Ya,' he said, and was quiet.

'I don't want to talk to you. Just get lost,' I said, lighting a cigarette rebelliously. I'd almost quit smoking under the pressure of his nagging.

'But why are you getting so angry with me? *I* didn't do anything.'

'Ya, but you never stop doing chaploosi to your "Jumboji", either.'

'So? I'm a struggling actor, I *have* to be nice to him.'

'Sure, you have to be nice to him, you have to run after him all the time, wagging your tail.'

'So what should I do, walk out of the film just because they've got a couple of whores on the set?' Rahul said, getting angry.

'When did I ever say that? When have I ever told you what you should or shouldn't do? Do what you want to do. Go, go to that air-conditioned van and fuck whichever dancer you like.'

'Thank you for your kind permission, Madam,' he said. 'You have such little faith in me, maybe I should fuck around. Just so as to prove you right.'

'So fine, go on. What stops you?'

'Because I don't *want* to,' he said angrily. 'You know me for four whole months now, but it still hasn't got into your stupid head that I'm not like Jumboji.'

'You might not *be* like your fucking "Jumboji", but you're too much into sucking up to him to even *suggest* that what he's doing is immoral.'

'You're so bloody holier-than-thou! Why don't you go and "suggest" to the pimps and prostitutes in Kamathipura that what they're doing is immoral?'

'I don't even know where Kamathipura is,' I muttered.

'Get into a local train, get off at Grant Road station, east side, and ask a taxi to take you to Kamathipura. I'm sure you'll find somebody to talk to. There are thousands of prostitutes there.'

'But Rahul, I work *here*, not in Kamathipura. I joined a film-making unit, not a whorehouse.'

'Our set doesn't turn into a whorehouse just because they've got three whores here today. Or even because they've been using the casting couch for casting the female artistes,' he said. 'We are making a film here and all of us have been working our asses off day and night to make that bloody film, not to service clients. I don't approve of

Jumboji's arranging for the AC van, but that has nothing to do with the actor-director relationship we share.'

'Great actor-director relationships we have in our unit. Mrignayani fucks Jumbo, and you lick his ass.'

Rahul walked out.

I'd cooled down by the time we got home, but Rahul was so furious, he refused to even talk to me. We got into bed and lay there, our backs to each other. Finally, I couldn't take it any longer and touched his shoulder. He threw the sheet off himself and walked out of the bedroom. I lay in bed for a while, then got up and followed him into the living room.

He was lying on the sofa, his feet dangling over the edge. I switched on the light in the passage so that the living room was lit by a soft, low light and sat near him on the ground. He turned his face away from me. I nibbled his ear.

'Has anybody told you that your ears are like Mr Spock's in *Star Trek*?' I whispered.

'Yes,' he said shortly.

'Oh,' I said, feeling a little bad. 'Who?'

'Jumboji's wife. I had to sleep with her to get the role, you know,' Rahul said sarcastically. 'She took one look at me and said, "Ooh, you've got shuch cutie-cutie ears. Like Mr Shpock in *Shtar Trek*." And then she ripped off my clothes and ravished me.'

'You've got shuch cutie-cutie ears,' I giggled, nuzzling his neck and biting his ear. 'I'm sho hungree. Please let me eat them, jusht a ittle-little...'

'Why do you want to sleep with a whore? That's what you think I am, don't you?' Rahul pushed me away and sat up. 'Oh, I'm so sorry. I forgot for a minute. You don't want to *sleep* with me. I'm not worthy of "going all the way" with.'

'Now look, don't mix up issues. I was disgusted with the AC van business and still am. But it wasn't right of me to take out my anger on you. I'm sorry about that. And about calling you a chaploos. But you don't have to take it so literally, na.'

'You don't think I'm a chaploos?' he countered.

'Well...' I said, choosing my words carefully.

'But it's true,' he said despondently. 'I *am* a chaploos. I have to be. I don't have an industry background, my father isn't financing my films. Unless a solo film of mine is a hit, I *have* to do P.R., don't you understand?'

'But your *Paapi* is doing well,' I said, putting my hand on his knee.

'Only in Delhi-Uttar Pradesh,' he said worriedly. 'It's a washout in Bombay territory. I'm not getting the kind of offers I thought I would. Other than Jumboji's film, I have only one film in hand. He might cast me in his next film as the main lead – he's fed up with Mehboob Khan's tantrums. I *have* to be in his next film, do you understand?'

'So you can't question anything he does, hm?' I said, looking out of the window at the neem tree swaying in the breeze.

'Why don't *you* question him?'

'I wouldn't know what to say. I mean, where do I begin? "You should respect your work enough not to make the actresses who want to work with you prostitute themselves"? It makes no sense,' I said. 'Maybe I will write something in my resignation letter, I don't know. I'm quitting. I don't want to stay around for the edit.'

'What will you do, then?'

'Look for a job in advertising,' I said.

'Maybe that's just as well.' He caressed my hair, then made a face and crossed his arms. 'I wish I could do something but... right now I have to go with the flow. I'm just a struggling actor... I have to do my P.R., otherwise I'll be just another flop, do you understand?' he said, sliding down from the sofa to sit by my side.

'Does it bother you, having to do chaploosi?' I said, holding his hand.

'Being nice to people comes naturally to me, that's not the hassle. But being nice with an agenda – it makes me feel so hypocritical sometimes, when I think about it. And you don't just have to be nice, you have to lick their boots if you want to get anything from them.'

'But does it actually work? Jumbo's so sharp, can't he see through your flattery?'

'Of course he can, but he doesn't mind. He thinks these perks of power are his due. He appreciates the fact that I've been trying so hard – I've even given up asking him what my character's motivation is. Manoj told me once that Jumboji was thinking of throwing me out of the film after the first week of shooting because I chewed his brain too much. But I've managed to get into Jumboji's good books now. I'm ninety per cent sure that he'll take me in his next film. He'll finalise the casting by December, so

I have four months to save up for my plastic surgery...'

'What plastic surgery?'

'For my ears.'

I was flabbergasted.

'Oh, but I love your ears,' I said.

'You do?' he said, touching his ears. 'But it's not just Jumboji, a lot of other people in the industry have also commented on them. I don't mind them myself, it's just that I don't want to lose any role because a producer or a director thinks they look funny. I have to maximise my chances every way. I wish I could tell these guys to get lost, but... Thank God, I'm not an actress, at least I don't have to sleep with anybody for roles,' he said.

'Uh...' I said, hesitant to even put my thoughts into words. 'Mrignayani said that even actors have to do it – all these gay producers...'

'God, no, I haven't done that,' he said, shocked. 'I've only licked ass.'

'Only,' I said, smiling.

'If my self-respect were more important to me than my ambition, I wouldn't be doing chaploosi this way. But I can't stand the thought of being a failure.'

'Hero or zero, hmm?'

'But I don't blame you for not respecting me,' he said. 'Sometimes I don't respect myself.'

'But I *do* respect you,' I said gently.

'You respect a chaploos?' he said, playing with the sleeve of my nighty.

'You're taking this too seriously, sweetheart – I told you, na, I wasn't angry with you to start off with. And anyway, you don't have to be perfect for me to respect you. Most of us have something we're ashamed of. Skeletons in our closet.'

'Where's your skeleton?' he said, looking up at me with a small smile.

I raised my arms and did a little skeleton-dance. 'Jangle, jangle, jangle.'

'Jingle, jingle, jingle,' he said and nuzzled my neck.

'I had an abortion once,' I said abruptly.

He looked up at me. 'With Karan?'

'Hm,' I said, looking at the neem tree outside the window. 'It was an accident and of course it wasn't possible to have the baby, so we... had an abortion.'

He put his arms around me.

'So, that's my skeleton,' I said, biting my cheeks from inside. 'Didn't expect a literal one, did you?'

He held me close and caressed my hair. 'Why don't you tell me about it?'

So I told him everything. All the details, right from the sweet-faced Malayali nurse who was so kind to me in the operation theatre that I almost changed my mind, to my feeling like a murderer when I saw the lumps of blood on my pad after the abortion. I even told him about how I couldn't separate my grief about the abortion from my feelings about Karan – it would have been *our* baby...

'You're crying?' Rahul said gently.

I shook my head. I wasn't crying, but I was shivering, and I hugged my knees tightly. Somehow, I'd never told anybody the details before. Not even Saira and Kavita. They'd probably not wanted to disturb me by asking questions.

'You know something, what I feel worst about is that I can't tell Ma. It's not just that she'd blow up at me – I could take that. But she'll feel so bad, so guilty that she sent me to Bombay and I had to go through all this.'

'How could Karan just call you up a week after you've had an abortion and tell you it's off?' Rahul said, agitated. 'If I ever meet him, I might just break his teeth. Or his jaw, better still.'

'My hero,' I said, and gave him a small smile as I put an arm around him. 'But it's not just Karan's fault. I'm responsible too. I could have had the baby all by myself. With my kind of background and Ma and all, it didn't seem very possible, but maybe – I don't know, if I *had* decided to have the baby, maybe things would have fallen into place. But what about the money, where would that have come from?'

'You could have continued to work for that production house,' Rahul said.

'Ya,' I said, putting my hand on my tummy. 'It would have been so nice, na?'

He also put his hand on my tummy and we sat together in the semi-darkness for a while, not talking, just hugging each other. Nobody can turn back the clock anyway, but an abortion is something you just can't undo. It felt nice all the same, thinking of what might have been.

'What about you,' I said with a smile, 'would you have fallen for me if I had a baby?'

'Sure. I'm very good at changing nappies.'

'You wouldn't mind me with some other man's baby?' I said.

'I wouldn't,' he said.

I didn't know whether he was telling the truth, but I felt comforted.

'How come you know how to change nappies?' I said.

'When I was thirteen, my cousin came to our place to have her first baby. She'd run away to marry a Muslim boy, so her father, that's Papa's older brother, refused to let her come to his house. All the men in my family are bloody tyrants.'

'But your Papa let her come to his place to have her baby,' I said, glad for the change in subject.

'Sure. That's because he's a Marxist, he was damn happy that she's married a Muslim. And he won't admit it, but he was damn kicked that his brother was so bugged with him about it. Papa loves to play politics.'

'Why do you dislike your father so much?' I said, shifting a little so that I could see his face.

'Well, I respect his principles, but I don't respect him, because he doesn't live up to them,' Rahul said. 'He likes to talk the talk about gender equality, but you should see the way he treats my mother.'

'So many men have double standards,' I said, shaking my head.

'I don't know how much of it is due to double standards,' Rahul said thoughtfully. 'I think he'd have been happier if he'd married some super-intellectual, well-read person. But Mama's a sweet, simple woman. She loves knitting and cooking – and he makes so much fun of her! He's the kind of person who'll walk over anybody who'll let him.'

'And you won't let him.'

'Definitely not,' Rahul said, pushing his chin out.

'Hmm,' I said, hiding my smile with a hand. 'You learnt cooking from your Mama?'

He nodded.

'It was very nice of you to help your cousin with the nappies and all,' I said.

'No,' he said, starting to smile. 'That wasn't because of niceness. I had this major crush on her ever since I was a kid. She was always beautiful, but after she had the baby, my God, she looked like a devi.'

'Oh, like that.'

'I'm telling you, Paro, she used to glow so much, it was like she had a zero-power bulb under her skin.'

I laughed, trying not to sound jealous.

'Where is she now?' I asked.

'Her husband works for the United Nations, so they live in New York. She sent me a really cute email after she saw *Maut Ke Sikandar*,' Rahul said happily. 'Her daughter wanted my autograph. She mustn't have seen *Paapi* yet. I'm sure she'll write.'

'Ya, ya. She'll see you've become a star and regret that she didn't fall for you then,' I said, jealousy creeping into my voice.

He looked at me quizzically.

'I won't mind if you're not successful,' I blurted out.

'Why?' he said, surprised.

'No...' I said vaguely, making a face. 'I mean, I'm happy with things as they are. And if you become a star, you'll have all these girls throwing themselves at you. I mean...'

'That's not why I want to be a star,' he protested. 'I'm not interested in all those things.'

'What about that girl in red?'

'Which girl...? Oh, that dancer! I was just appreciating the way she was dancing, baba, nothing else.'

'Oh, that's all, huh? She'd got such a great body.'

'Really? I didn't notice,' he said, eyes twinkling.

'Do you think I'm fat?' I asked abruptly.

'I think you're gorgeous,' he said, and proceeded to convince me of the same. Not in words.

'Has he proposed to you?' Kavita asked.

'No, not proposed as such,' I said, biting into my salad. I'd recently started watching the calories. 'But he keeps on talking about things like farmer's wife and all.'

Kavita looked at me sceptically. I wanted to avoid looking at her without making it obvious, so I gave a warm smile to the waiter who'd brought a Diet Coke for Saira.

'Madam, milkshake for you?' he said.

'No, not today,' I said regretfully.

I took a sip of Saira's Diet Coke and made a face.

'You know something, at a political level, I think this "thin is in" business is damn dumb,' I said. 'But it's just that my ass looks so big nowadays.'

Kavita refused to be sidetracked.

'Has Rahul said that he loves you?' she said.

'Well, he has mentioned it a couple of times, you know, like, when we're in bed. And he keeps on singing all these love songs to me.'

'Oh, that doesn't mean anything,' Kavita said. 'I don't understand how you could just start living with...'

'But what could I do?' I defended myself. 'There was nowhere else...'

'What about now?'

'I'm very busy with my job-hunting, but I am searching for a place as well. I really am, don't look at me like that.'

'Forget about proposals-voposals, guys,' Saira broke in. 'A man who does the cooking is not to be scoffed at.'

'Anyway, how does it matter. We're just having an affair,' I said. 'Enjoy!'

'But *what* are you enjoying, yaar?' Saira said. 'Both of you must end up highly frustrated.'

'Uh, not necessarily... "Everything But" is much more fun than I thought it would be. And you know something,' I was blushing, but I had to tell them, 'when we're... together, he's more bothered that I enjoy myself than that he... you know.'

'Oh, so he's a good lover,' Kavita said. 'Smart guy. He knows that if you enjoy yourself, you'll keep on coming back for more, so...'

I sniffed with impatience. I was starting to get a little bugged by Kavita's attitude.

'Waiter,' I called. 'One pav bhaji.' I figured that the salad I'd had would compensate for the calories in the pav bhaji.

'But this whole "Everything But" business,' Kavita said hesitantly. 'Is it because you're scared of getting pregnant or something?'

'No, not really,' I said, taking a sip of my non-diet Pepsi. 'I know enough about contraception, that's not really a hassle, it's just that… not going all the way makes me feel a little safer emotionally. I want to keep a distance.'

'And what about him, doesn't he have a problem with your "no going all the way" funda?' Saira said.

'Ya,' I said. 'He grumbles.'

'I don't know, but somehow, I find it a bit fishy, the way he goes along with whatever you say,' Kavita said. 'Is he a wimp or something? Doesn't the man have a backbone?'

'Or a frontbone,' Saira added, giggling.

'What do you mean?' I said, indignant. 'He's a *nice* guy.'

'I think I agree with Kavita about the wimp business,' Saira said.

'Both of you are fine ones to talk,' I said angrily. 'Your boyfriends treat you like dirt, and you think that's the way relationships have to be. I find a nice guy, you try to put him down.'

'I didn't know that I have to lead a perfect life myself in order to qualify for giving advice to my friends,' Kavita sniffed.

The waiter served me my pav bhaji and I attacked it, but even the taste of buttered pav and bhaji wasn't enough to soothe me.

'Anyway, we don't need each other to figure out how we should run our lives,' I said.

But it wasn't really true. I didn't know why it was so important to me that they agreed with me. That they saw my point of view, at least. I looked away, then looked back at them.

'I'm really very sorry I talked that way about your boyfriends,' I said. 'Of course I need your opinions and advice but... but, don't you understand? It's that pattern stuff Kavita's shrink keeps on talking about.'

'What pattern stuff?' Saira said, looking confused.

'That we have a pattern of getting involved with unavailable men who treat us badly. We find nice guys boring while the bastards seem very attractive... Am I getting it right, Kavita?'

Kavita nodded.

'But imagine having to spend all your life with a boring, unattractive guy,' Saira said.

'Rahul isn't boring *or* unattractive,' I said.

'I see your point, but isn't your Rahul a bit *too* nice?' Kavita said thoughtfully. 'I mean, is he for real?'

'He did admit to me that he's nice to everybody on the sets so that he gets more work out of them,' I said, starting to get worried. 'He could be playing a chocolate-lover for me. How would I know? He is a professional actor, after all.'

'Hey, don't take it so seriously. I didn't want to upset you,' Kavita rushed to say, seeing the dejection on my face.

'No... I mean, it's OK,' I said. 'You'd warned me about Karan and I'd just blown up at you. It was only after the abortion happened that I realised you were right all along...'

'Forget about all that,' Kavita said quietly.

'Ya, I know, what's the point,' I said, making a face.

'Why do you want to get her depressed?' Saira said angrily to Kavita. 'She was so happy when she walked in.'

'It's not just Kavita. Obviously I also have my reservations about Rahul, that's why I keep on... holding back,' I said, toying with the radish on my plate. 'But sometimes, I want to believe, I so much want to believe.'

'Maybe he is the real thing, who knows?' Kavita said.

'Rahul's so eager-to-please, he's like a puppy. It feels so different, somehow,' I paused uncertainly, 'to have somebody else being so nice to me for a change. Karan never treated me badly as such, but I was always the one who was running after him. Sometimes I... wish that I could be nicer to Rahul. All he knows is this scared child inside me, who's been hurt and keeps on trying to run away. He doesn't know how much I can love him, how much I can give...'

'Then maybe you should be nice to him,' Kavita said gently. 'What stops you?'

I made a face, then told them, 'A couple of days back I saw a really cute plant in a nursery and bought it for Rahul's place. Then, when I got home, I started thinking about what it *meant* – setting down roots and all... My God, it was so fucking symbolic, it really grossed me out.'

'What did you do with the plant, finally?'

'I put it outside the front door,' I said sheepishly. 'It looks quite nice on the landing, actually.'

Kavita looked at me, shaking her head. 'I'm telling you, Paro, you're going to get hurt. I'm telling you... I think I should just shut up.'

I made a face and tied my hair back tightly. 'I'll be fine.'

'I'm sure you will,' Kavita said, patting my hand. 'I should be concentrating on sorting out my own life, but I just can't help worrying about the two of you.'

'She'll be fine,' Saira said, taking a sip of my Pepsi. 'By the way, what's happening with your shrink, Kavita?'

'I've achieved some really important insights into my Electra complex,' Kavita said. 'The therapy's in a critical phase now, but I've had to take a break for a while – my shrink's come down with bronchitis.'

'Whacko says that all physical diseases are manifestations of imbalances in a person's emotional life,' Saira said. 'I can't remember about bronchitis... Oh yes, lung problems happen to people who, deep down, want to stop interacting with other people.'

Kavita gave her a look.

'He just read it somewhere,' Saira backtracked.

'How are things with Whacko?' I asked.

'Well, I'm trying to break up with him. I know what you must be thinking, but I really am. It's just that he says sorry so cutely...' Saira said helplessly.

Kavita refused to say anything.

'Uh... How is he otherwise?' I said, trying to fill in the silence.

'He's OK. I mean he was OK till just a couple of days back. He's cut down completely on the hash – he's been smoking only one joint a day for the past three weeks. Then he ran into a bunch of his old buddies and they talked him into trying crystal meth. But the next morning he got such a terrible hangover, he just couldn't take it – he broke all the chinaware in his house. Not that he had much china, only three plates and...'

'God, what do I do with these girls?' Kavita said, holding her head in her hands.

I was in bed with Rahul when the phone rang.

He picked up the phone and said hello in the deep baritone voice that was meant to impress producers into furnishing dotted lines and signing amounts.

'It's for you,' he said.

I took a deep breath and said, 'Hello?'

'Paro?' Saira said. 'I'm at Whacko's place, tell me quick why I need to break up with him, I need a booster dose of antibodies, quick, before he comes back from the loo.'

'I... Right. One, he's got a violent temper. Two, he does drugs. Three, he says he loves you but he keeps on meeting his ex-girlfriend. Four... four, ya, four, you can't find someone nice till you dump him. Five, he's not...'

'Whacko's back. Bye!'

'Bye-bye, best of luck!' I put the receiver down and turned around – to see Rahul looking at me, astounded.

FIFTEEN

'Good morning, good morning, great to be alive!' Rahul sang, bounding out of bed early in the morning, full of pep and cheer. I sank deep into the quilt, shutting out the sun. How could anybody be so disgustingly happy so early in the morning?

'Get up, you lazy pig!' he shouted, trying to pull the covers off me.

'Grawk!' I croaked, holding on to my quilt. 'Go and make me some breakfast.'

I'd barely managed to close my eyes when he was back. If he hadn't been holding a tray with breakfast in it, I wouldn't have believed that he'd ever been away.

'Look, I'm blissfully bekaar, I don't have to get up,' I grumbled. 'I'll eat it later.'

'You've got an appointment,' he said.

'At twelve o'clock. Let me sleep,' I said and drew the covers over my head.

He tugged the quilt but I held on tightly. I was wide awake now but I refused to get up, on a matter of principle.

He retreated into the bathroom, complaining loudly about lazy pigs who were soon going to turn into hogs. I closed my eyes and smiled, not understanding what he was talking about and not particularly interested in figuring it out either. The soft sound of the shower lulled me and I was about to doze off, when he grabbed my quilt and jerked it off me.

'That's unfair,' I complained and curled into a ball on the bed, mewling like a kitten.

He seemed moved by pity, or something else, because he changed his mind and returned the quilt to the bed – along with himself.

'I won,' I giggled. 'Hey, let go of my T-shirt.'

'It's *my* T-shirt,' he said. 'I want it back.'

'Your name isn't written on it,' I said, laughing, but by that time, he'd already tugged it off me. 'Hey, give it back...'

He shut me up with a kiss, but what with all that his hands were doing to me, I didn't mind too much. Almost of their own volition, my legs parted and hugged him.

'You feel so good,' he murmured. 'So warm and...'

By the time I realised what was happening, he was almost inside me. I pushed him away gently. 'No, na, baby, hmm?'

'Baby, baby,' he whispered, not letting me go. 'Please...'

'We'd agreed,' I said, kissing him lightly and pushing him away.

'But that was such a long time ago,' he said, putting my arms around his neck and snuggling into me. 'Ya, trust me. Let me fuck you. Let me love you, sweetheart, open up to me, why don't you...'

He was kissing me passionately by now, while I was trying to maintain my cool.

'Rahul, Rahul, please wait, baby, I'd said, hadn't I...'

'Ya, "you'd said", "you'd said",' he shouted, suddenly furious.

He threw the quilt off both of us and sat up in bed. I tied my hair into a knot and reached out for his T-shirt which was lying on the bedside table.

'Look,' I said, after I had put it on. We'd argued about this before, but I'd never seen him get so angry. 'I understand what...'

'You don't understand a thing,' he said, getting off the bed and starting to put on his clothes. 'Or, no. Maybe you do understand. Maybe you get your kicks teasing me.'

'That's not true,' I protested. 'Just because we want different...'

'Sure. And your wants are the only ones that matter, right? You're so bloody self-centred. All you've done in this relationship is take, take, take. I'm the one who cooks for you, who cheers you up when you're down, who's always there for you whenever you need me.'

I started to smile. 'You think I should have sex with you because you cook for me, what?'

'You have the intelligence of an ant. No, why should I insult ants? Less, much less than an ant.'

He was getting really mad, so I bit my cheeks from inside and tried to look serious. 'I'm sorry about what I said about cooking and sex. I take it back.'

'Why the fuck should you take it back? That's what you feel, don't you, Paro? That I'm doing all this for you just so as to get you. That I'm just a dog, salivating over your body. God, you make me feel so cheap for wanting you.'

I started to say something, but he interrupted me again. 'You're treating me like shit just because I don't behave badly in turn. Ya, it's time the worm turned.'

'What worm, Rahul, now don't get dramatic.'

'Go on, put me down, put me down some more,' he shouted at me. 'I'm just a dumb Hindi film actor, amn't I, not a hi-fi cinematographer.'

'Don't drag Karan into this discussion,' I snapped, my sense of humour receding. 'It's got nothing to do with him.'

'Oh ya? Then what's the problem? I don't turn you on, huh?' he said sarcastically, pulling on his socks.

'No, you do, it's just that...'

'It's not like you're a bloody fucking virgin or something.'

'How can you... What do you mean?'

'Nothing,' he said, and sat down on the corner of the bed, holding his head in his hands.

'Are you crying?' I asked hesitantly.

He looked up at me, giving me a tired smile.

'I don't know what the hell he has that I don't,' he said helplessly. 'That you're still so caught up with him.'

'That's not really true,' I said.

'He's always there. Always present. At the back of your mind. You're always comparing, aren't you?'

'No I'm not, not like... *that*.'

'No, I'm not talking about like that, not about bed, at least I presume you don't.' He stopped for a second. I reached out to touch his hand, but he snapped it back, furious. 'What the hell do I know? I keep on thinking that you must've had this great sex life with him, but maybe you were so bloody stuck-up with him too.'

'How dare you?' I shouted, losing my temper. I'd been allowing him to blow off steam, but this was too bloody much. 'It's none of your bloody fucking business.'

'How dare you do this and how dare you do that,' he mimicked in a girlish voice. 'I should just be a good little boy and do only what I'm supposed to, huh?'

'There are two of us in this relationship, dammit, you can't force me to open up to you till *I* feel like. It's my fucking choice, how far I want to go with you.'

'And I just have to lump it whether I like it or not, right?'

'I'm not holding a gun to your head and forcing you to be with me,' I spat out. 'If you don't want to be with me on these terms, you're free to fuck off.'

'I've taken enough,' Rahul said. 'I can't go on like this.'

We were both of us silent for a while, then I said, 'I'm sorry. I didn't really *mean...*'

'*I* mean it. Either you're with me completely or it's over,' he said, and walked out of the room.

'You'll have to wait for half an hour,' the harried secretary said. 'Mr Ramchandani is busy in a meeting.'

'No problem,' I said and smiled, although Mr Ramchandani had barked into the phone while giving me an appointment – 'Twelve o'clock sharp. I don't like latecomers.' I was the one who needed a job, not he.

I sat on the highly-fashionable but highly-uncomfortable wooden couch, tapping the floor with my heel. Then I realised what I was doing and made myself stop. I took out a cigarette but just as I was lighting up, I saw a 'This is not a Joke, You will kill me with your Smoke,' sign on the wall, and quickly ground it out in the pack.

I checked my watch. Three minutes after twelve. I thought of calling up Rahul on his mobile. But he usually switched off his mobile when he was working, even if it was just a rehearsal. And anyway, what would I say to him?

I wondered whether I was giving too much importance to this fight. Rahul and I had fought before and we'd made up. But what if this was the last straw, what if Rahul really did walk out on me? I wouldn't blame him if he did. It wasn't just the 'Everything But' business. I'd put up rules, boundaries everywhere, like our relationship were a game.

I thought of calling up Kavita or Saira, but no, this was a decision I had to make myself. I took a sheet of paper out of my bag and divided it into two. On one side I wrote down all the reasons why I felt that Rahul was worthy of trust. I started with his thoughtfulness and ended up with seven points in all. My pen paused at the top of the 'Cons' column. Why should I not trust him? 'He's an actor,' I wrote. He seemed to be a nice enough person, but the 'seemed' was extremely important. What if he was only acting? My judgement had fucked up once – what if I fucked up again?

Half an hour later, I had a neat little chart in my hand. The logic was all laid out, but the balance was stuck firmly in the middle. I didn't know how to decide. What about my heart, my feelings?

I closed my eyes and asked myself what I wanted. 'To be with Rahul.' And what stopped me? 'I'm scared.' Brilliant. Fat lot of help my feelings were.

I took out a coin from my bag. Heads, I'd let down my defences. Tails, I'd let him walk away from me if he chose to. I tossed the coin and caught it. I stared at my closed hand, heart thudding. What did I want it to be? What if it were tails, would I let Rahul go, just like that?

I started to open my hand, then shut it with a snap and thrust the coin back into my purse. Rahul didn't deserve his fate being decided by the toss of a coin, he'd been much too nice to me, much too loving and tolerant of all my idiosyncrasies and defences, much too...

I got up and walked out of the office into the crowded street.

'Satyam Dance Hall, Juhu?' I asked an auto driver.

He nodded, looking at me strangely as I got in.

'Everything OK, Madam?' he asked, peering at my reflection in the rear-view mirror.

'What?' I said, and touched my face – to realise that I was crying.

'Everything's alright,' I said, wiping my face. Everything was alright now.

'Ghunghat ke pat khol ri, tohe piya milenge,' Kabir sang. *Open your veil and you will see your Beloved*. I had opened my veil and I was off, to meet my piya. Riding in a rickety, mud-splattered auto-rickshaw down the potholed streets of Bombay. I laughed a bit, but I had to press my trembling lips with my hand not to start crying again. I'd been so, so dumb. I'd been wearing my cynicism like yellow-coloured glasses, letting it jaundice my view of everything and everyone around. I'd been making Rahul pay for what Karan had done. And if that wasn't enough, even for what Jumbo and Manoj and Mrignayani were doing. It was time to forgive Karan, not for his sake, but so that I could be free.

Rahul was right. There was a world of love and security waiting for me, if only I'd open myself to it. And I would. Let down my defences and love him and make up for all the...

'Madam,' the auto driver said hesitantly, tapping the metre. 'Twenty-seven rupees.'

I checked my watch as I half-walked, half-ran down the corridor. Rahul had told me that they usually broke for lunch at about one o'clock, so if I was lucky, I could catch him before that.

'Madam, rehearsal is on,' the spot boy in front of the rehearsal room door said, trying to stop me.

'Rahul Kapoor's rehearsal, na? No problem,' I said, side-stepping him.

'Madam please...' the spot said.

I opened the door and froze. Rahul was standing with his back to me, passionately kissing a woman's neck as she arched back...

I let the door swing shut and just stood there, not knowing what to do.

'Madam, I told you,' the spot boy whined.

'Ya, you told me,' I said blankly.

SIXTEEN

It was like something out of a film, it was that classic, I thought, laughing hysterically.

'Have you left a note for him?' Saira asked.

'A note...' I said vaguely. 'No. It doesn't seem... necessary.'

I picked up my bags and cast one final look behind me, thinking, 'Have I forgotten to take anything with me?'

I remembered all the times when I'd left Rahul's place, checking whether I'd taken the key. I laughed or cried, I'm not sure which, and shook my head. Taking a deep, long, shaky breath, I took his key out of my bag, tossed it on the floor, and closed the door behind me.

There were no 'I-told-you-so's. That's the nicest thing about friends. Not that their practical help was any less, either. Saira cajoled, pleaded, and threatened her landlady into letting me stay at her place. Kavita called up at least twice a day and brought my favourite Black Forest pastries along whenever she came to visit. But I didn't feel like eating anything.

I didn't go out of the house, didn't do anything, just stayed in bed all day, crying, like I had after my abortion. I couldn't understand how I'd found myself in this situation all over again. I'd thought that I was being so smart, but it didn't hurt any less because it'd all been so casual, because we were 'just having an affair'. My defences hadn't even prevented me from falling in love with Rahul.

But maybe it wasn't really love, maybe it was... a kind of attachment. Just an attachment, that's all. Of course, I had enjoyed the physical part of our relationship, and I missed that. That was natural, of course it was. And it was just as natural that I missed the way he made me laugh. Anybody would. And that my stomach, which was bunched up all the time, turned every time the neighbour called out to her son. Why did Rahul have to be such a common name?

Just an attachment, that's all. I remembered how some superglue had stuck to my hand when I was working on the sets for Mr Bose. I'd pulled it off with a jerk and the skin had come off with it. I couldn't believe it, couldn't do anything except stare at the white flesh getting streaked with blood that dripped on my jeans.

Had it hurt more when Karan had left me? It had been a different kind of pain. I'd felt devastated, just crumbled up within. It had changed my way of looking at the world, changed me as a person. This time I just felt this relentless need to go back to Rahul, to climb up the stairs to his place, running up the last few steps, opening the door... But no, I'd left the key behind, so I'd ring the bell and he'd open the door and I'd throw myself into his arms and we'd both be crying and laughing and holding each other tight and...

I sat down and had an honest, heart-to-heart talk with myself. What the fuck was the point of lying? Yes, I did love Rahul. Maybe Kavita was right, maybe my falling for him was just a part of my pattern of falling for unavailable men, but if I underestimated my feelings for him, I'd be slipping in my resolve and going back to him before I knew it myself. I'd read somewhere that it takes more fuel for a rocket to fly the first six thousand kilometres from the earth's surface, than it does to go the rest of the distance to the moon. Of course I would feel like going back to him, it was only to be expected, but I had to use my will power as the fuel, otherwise I'd end up crash-landing again.

Labels don't matter, actions do, I told myself, and resolutely pulled out a list of production houses that I had to call up for a job. I was making my fifth call of the day, speaking to a production designer Sharmishtha had told me to contact, when the doorbell rang. I requested him to hold on, and went and opened the door to see – who else but our hero, Rahul Kapoor.

'I knew you'd land up here eventually,' I said dryly.

He'd dressed for the part, I noted – ragged blue jeans, a crumpled shirt, a two-day stubble, and yes, even a mad glint in the eyes.

I hadn't forgotten that the production designer was on the line, I told him politely that I would call him up later and put the phone down. Good. This was going well. Except for a raised heartbeat, I was in complete control of myself.

'Let's go and sit in Saira's room,' I told Rahul. 'And keep your voice low. If Saira's landlady wakes up because of your shouting, she'll chuck her out.'

I followed him into Saira's room and closed the door behind me. But didn't bolt it. I hoped that he got the hint. He sat on the bed. I sat on the chair which was furthest away from him. Act cool, I told myself.

'It's a very... pink room,' he said, taking in the pink walls and bedspread and cushions and curtains.

'Yes, it is.'

'Kavita said that you don't want to talk to me,' he said abruptly.

'Ya, I don't,' I said. Kavita hadn't told me about his calling her up – she must've wanted to protect me from temptation. 'How come you knew her phone number?'

'You'd called her once from my mobile,' he said.

I refused to ask him how he had found out where I was staying. It would just give him one more opportunity to show off.

'Look.' He cleared his throat. 'I'm really sorry about blowing up at you. I take back everything I said. We can continue doing "Everything But" for all our lives, I don't mind.'

'What?' I said.

'It's OK, bhai, no hassles. I won't even talk about going all the way,' he said, trying to smile. 'We'll be the "Everything But" champions of the country. The answer to India's population problems.'

'No, I'm not angry about that,' I said curtly. 'I'd forgiven you for the fight, I was even... Forget about all that.'

'Great. Forget about it. Come back.'

'And what about Rashmi?'

'What about her?'

Oh, so the bastard hadn't even realised that I'd seen him. I felt like chucking him out of the house, but I knew that I would have to have this talk with him sometime or the other, so I told him.

'Oh my poor baby,' he said, rushing to take me in his arms.

'Don't you... I'll scream, I'll shout, you'll be responsible if the neighbours call the police.'

'Calm down, calm down,' he said, moving back. 'It's just a misunderstanding. We'll have it cleared up in a minute.'

'What fucking misunderstanding?'

'What you saw was just a rehearsal,' he announced.

'Don't give me shit. You need to rehearse for a kiss?'

'There's no lip-to-lip kiss happening, baba. She's wearing all this jewellery, like Rekha in *Utsav*. I'm supposed to take it off with my teeth, OK? I kiss her neck and take off her necklace, kiss her waist, take off her kamarbandh, kiss her foot, take off her anklet. We had to work out how much time we'd take for each — to set it to the music.'

I was stumped.

'What bullshit,' I said finally.

'The choreographer was there, his assistant was there. Hey, come on, baba, even if I wanted to kiss her, would I do it in front of so many people? Huh?'

'I didn't see anybody.'

'How...? OK, ya, they were sitting near the music system, you couldn't have seen them from the door.' He stuffed his hand into his pockets and tapped his foot. 'Right. You can call up the choreographer and ask...'

'What are you talking about, setting it to music, hah! You were kissing her neck for a good five seconds, minimum, when I saw you.'

'Right, so the song lasts for three minutes, thirty-six seconds. The kissing business happens during the sections when there is just instrumental music, because, obviously, I can't be kissing her while I'm singing. The first interlude is for twelve seconds – four for taking off her necklace, eight for kissing her neck. The second interlude is twelve seconds – six for taking off her kamarbandh, six for...'

'You have all the maths down pat, huh?' I said.

'Of course I do. That's what we were doing all day. The rehearsal packed up at ten o'clock in the night. And when I come back home, you're gone, all your stuff's gone, your key's on the floor – I went mad.'

'Hello?' I said, thinking of something else. 'You'd told me that they're going to picturise the song as a slow dance. You never told me about this jewellery and kissing business before. Why was that, huh, tell me?'

'Because they changed the concept, they told me this new concept only after I'd reached the rehearsal hall in the morning.'

'You've got answers for everything,' I said. 'Aha, now I get it. The spot boy must have told you, you must have worked it all out before coming to meet me.'

'What spot boy?'

'The one at the door. He didn't want to let me in.'

'How is he supposed to know that you are my girlfriend?' Rahul argued. 'What would he tell me?'

'OK, so... so, you must have improvised your lines right now.'

'God, what did I ever do to deserve a woman like you?'

'Your God has let you off the hook now. Go. Go find some other woman,' I sneered. 'No, why find? She must be waiting for you, that what's-her-name, Rashmi. Mrignayani has told me lots of stories about her.'

'What's that got to do with me? I'm not even attracted to her.'

'You said that about Mrignayani also.'

'Right, I did, so? Did I ever have anything to do with her?'

'How would I know?'

He shook his head vigorously, then held up his hands. 'OK. We are to have this proper, rational discussion. I am not going to lose my temper. So – we're shooting this song on the sixteenth, you come to the set and watch, OK?'

'You can tell the director to put in this kissing from neck to foot business. He'll probably be happy to oblige you. More masala for him.'

'Come on, you've worked as an assistant director, how can you talk like some girl from a village? It was a rehearsal, for God's sake.'

'I've worked here, that's why I know exactly what the industry is like,' I said. 'I know what all goes on here.'

'You could call up Rashmi and speak to her, but no, I might have told her to lie. You could speak to the choreographer, but no, same problem,' he said, ticking off the possibilities. 'Hey, man, you tell me now, what proof do you want?'

'Nothing.' I shrugged.

'What the fuck do you mean – "nothing"? You're not even interested in the evidence, you're sitting on your great grand pedestal and you've already passed judgement, huh?'

I shrugged again.

'Hey, man, this is not fair. We're having a conversation, that means an exchange of ideas, right? You're so completely stuck.'

'OK, so there's a possibility that you're lying and a possibility that you're not,' I conceded. 'Neither of us can prove it either way, so, now...'

'So, now?'

'I don't believe you. It's as simple as that.'

'Oh, fuck. Your old trust-wala funda.'

'Exactly. My old trust-wala funda.'

'So what should I do now?'

'That's up to you, how would I know? As for the two of us – of course it's over.'

He hit the wall with his fist. 'I can't believe this. I can't fucking believe that you can leave me for such a stupid, stupid reason. After all I've done... I kept on thinking, let her have her "one-off" date, let her have her "just an affair". She's been hurt, it'll take her some time, but she'll fall in love with me...'

'I'm not in love with you,' I said. 'I realised it after I left you. Of course, there was a lot of physical attraction, and we got along well, so I'd started thinking that it was love, but...'

He grabbed my arms and shook me. 'You're so, so dumb, it's fucking incredible. You don't realise it, but you love me.'

'Hah! Like hell I do,' I shouted back at him.

'And what about me, what do you think, I've just been putting on all this while? Don't pretend you don't know how desperately I love you.'

'I think you're a very good actor.'

'Do you know what I've gone through in the past six days? I haven't even...'

'You deserve a Filmfare Award for Best Actor,' I told him.

'Now that I've found you, I'm not going to let you go. Don't think...'

'A National Award,' I shouted him down. 'You think you can fucking...'

'I'm fed up with...' He stopped abruptly.

'Ya, ya, go on, why did you stop?' I shouted at him. 'If you're so bloody fed up with me, why don't you...'

'Paro,' he whispered, looking over my shoulder.

'What?' I whirled around – to see Saira's landlady standing in the door. She gave me one look and left, banging the door behind herself.

'Oh my God,' I whispered.

'I'm sorry,' he said, letting me go.

'Oh shit, I hope she doesn't throw Saira out because of this.'

'Is Saira allowed to have male guests?' he whispered.

'In the daytime, yes, but a tamasha like this – God knows what'll happen.'

'I'm terribly sorry,' he said.

I folded the newspapers that were lying on the chair, then said, 'Actually, it's not your fault.'

'No, it is, you had told me not to raise my voice, but...'

'I wasn't talking about now. About this whole thing – it's not your fault. I have to take responsibility for my choices if I want to make better ones,' I told him. 'I subconsciously chose a partner who'd let me down. I set myself up for it.'

'What?' he said, nonplussed. 'Why would you do that?'

'It all goes back to the time when my father died. I was just seven years old then. I was the youngest daughter and his favourite and... I felt abandoned, somehow, like he'd "left" me by dying.'

'I'm sorry,' Rahul said.

'No, that's not the issue. You probably know about the Electra complex, don't you?'

'Uh... I've forgotten.'

'Well, girls fall in love with their fathers and subconsciously choose men who are similar to them. I felt that my father had left me, so I subconsciously chose to get involved with unavailable guys like Karan and you. Kavita says it's even possible that I knew all along, not consciously of course, that Karan was two-timing me.'

'Have you been going to a psychiatrist for all this?' he said, a little intimidated.

'No, but I plan to. When I have the money.'

'How do you know all this, then?'

'Kavita's been going to a shrink and she's told me all about it. Of course, my case is a little different from hers, but we've sat together and figured it out,' I told him. 'Anyway, our analysis makes sense, doesn't it?'

'Ya, I guess,' he said. Then, after a moment, 'Hey, no, it doesn't. I'm not unavailable.'

I stared at him, biting my lower lip.

'Look,' he said, 'I don't know anything about this psychology business. I mean, maybe you did get involved with Karan because of this Electra Complex thing. Maybe he did two-time you, but I haven't. If you're still in love with him, if that's the real reason you don't want me...'

'Well, in the beginning, I did get involved with you so as to get over Karan,' I began, but broke off when I saw the hurt in his eyes. 'I'm sorry...'

'No, no, it's OK, it's perfectly fine. I always knew it. What's the big deal,' he said, shrugging. 'Go on.'

'It doesn't make much sense, but my whole "let's just have an affair" funda and all...' I said slowly. 'I wasn't aware of it then, but it was the kind of relationship I thought Karan would have been happy with. Happy as in, he wouldn't have left me.'

'Do you... still want to go back to him?'

'No, not any more. That's over now, completely.'

'Then why don't you love me?' he said, holding my hands. 'I love you, we'll be so happy together. I'll never leave you like your Daddy did, I promise.'

I wouldn't cry, I told myself. Just wouldn't.

I burst into tears.

'Don't you dare,' I said, moving away as he tried to hold me in his arms. 'And don't think that just because I'm crying, I'm in love with you. Like that stupid "has gayi to phas gayi" business.'

'You are the one who keeps on coming up with all these Hindi film dialogues,' he said, watching helplessly as I sobbed into the pink curtain. The curtain, because there was no other cloth around, even my sleeves were too short. 'Hey, don't cry.'

He took out a crumpled packet of tissues from his pocket and gave me one.

'Oh, so now you're such a ladies man that you even carry around handkerchiefs with you,' I said, and blew my nose. 'Give me one more.'

'Why should I?' he said, but gave me the tissue. 'Has it ever occurred to you that I might be crying sometimes?'

'Ya, sure, glycerine costs ten rupees a bottle.'

'What do I do with you?' he said, and took me in his arms.

I struggled for a while, then let him hold me, but didn't put my arms around him.

'You'll try all these tactics, I know it, but I just have to ignore them if I have to get to the moon,' I reminded myself.

'What's this "getting to the moon" business?' he said.

I explained about the rocket fuel and the first six thousand kilometres to the moon.

'I'll take you to the moon, baby,' he said, the grin coming back, not in full strength, but coming back all the same.

'There you go again, with your Hindi film dialogues.'

'But goddammit, the moon was your idea,' he said, much aggrieved.

'I'm sorry,' I said.

'You should be,' he said, kissing my eyebrow.

'What if Saira's landlady comes back?' I said. 'She'll chuck her out.'

'Saira can shift in with us, no problem,' he said confidently.

'With "us"?' I said archly. 'What makes you assume that I will go back with you?'

'Come back home with me, sweetheart,' he said, nuzzling my hair. 'Home isn't home without you.'

'Kya dialogue hai! Taaliyaan!' I said, moving back and smiling. 'You're like candyfloss. A little sugar, lots of gloss. No substance.'

'Substance, substance...' he said, scratching his head. 'OK, ya, how about getting married, what do you say, will you marry me?'

'Marry you? Hah!' I said, buttoning up his shirt till the collar. 'You'd said once that you can't get married because struggling actors earn peanuts.'

'So we'll eat just peanuts,' he said, laughing with abandon. '"A book of verses beneath the bough, A jug of wine, a loaf of bread – and thou, Beside me, singing in the wilderness, Oh, wilderness were paradise enow!" Anyway, peanuts are very good for health. So, how about it, will you marry me?'

'Ya, now I get it, you'll make me work and support you while you struggle.'

'Brilliant idea,' he said, grinning.

I took a pen out of his shirt pocket and wrote my name on his jaw, then rubbed it out.

'You're underage,' I pointed out. 'If I marry you before you're twenty-one, I'll have to go to jail.'

'No big deal,' he said. 'What all sacrifices women have made for love – look at Juliet and Laila and Ranjha – or is it Heer? I always get confused who's the woman. All of them died for love. And look at you – scared of six months in jail.'

'And you will be roaming around scot-free!'

'I'll come and visit you in jail. I'll slip cigarettes to you through the bars, OK?' he said, nibbling my ear. 'Hey, what's the matter, don't cry.'

'Why should I be crying?' I said. And burst into tears.

'Baby, baby, OK, nobody's going to send my baby to jail,' he said, cradling me in his arms.

'I'm not crying because of that,' I said, hitting him and laughing through my tears.

'Why are you crying, then?'

'I love you,' I said. 'But I'm not completely sure.'

'What are you waiting for?' he said, smiling into my eyes. 'What's going to happen – there's going to be an announcement from the skies, or some big fluorescent cards are going to appear behind me, saying, "He is the One for You!"'

'I guess there are no guarantees in life, but... but what if you leave me some day?' I said.

'No, I won't,' he said.

'How do I know for sure?' I mumbled into his shirt.

'You know because you know.'

I raised my head and looked into his eyes, and realised that deep within me, I did know.

'Yes I will,' I said softly, putting my arms around him, 'come back home with you.'